The Father of British Canada: A Chronicle of Carleton

William Wood

Edited by George M. Wrong and H. H. Langton

CONTENTS

CHAPTER I

GUY CARLETON 1724-1759

Guy Carleton, first Baron Dorchester, was born at Strabane, County Tyrone, on the 3rd of September 1724, the anniversary of Cromwell's two great victories and death. He came of a very old family of English country gentlemen which had migrated to Ireland in the seventeenth century and intermarried with other Anglo-Irish families equally devoted to the service of the British Crown. Guy's father was Christopher Carleton of Newry in County Down. His mother was Catherine Ball of County Donegal. His father died comparatively young; and, when he was himself fifteen, his mother married the rector of Newry, the Reverend Thomas Skelton, whose influence over the six step-children of the household worked wholly for their good.

At eighteen Guy received his first commission as ensign in the 25th Foot, then known as Lord Rothes' regiment and now as the King's Own Scottish Borderers. At twenty-three he fought gallantly at the siege of Bergen-op-Zoom. Four years later (1751) he was a lieutenant in the Grenadier Guards. He was one of those quiet men whose sterling value is appreciated only by the few till some crisis makes it stand forth before the world at large. Pitt, Wolfe, and George II all recognized his solid virtues. At thirty he was still some way down the list of lieutenants in the Grenadiers, while Wolfe, two years his junior in age, had been four years in command of a battalion with the rank of lieutenant-colonel. Yet he had long been 'my friend Carleton' to Wolfe, he was soon to become one of 'Pitt's Young Men, ' and he was enough of a 'coming man' to incur the king's displeasure. He had criticized the Hanoverians; and the king never forgave him. The third George 'gloried in the name of Englishman. ' But the first two were Hanoverian all through. And for an English guardsman to disparage the Hanoverian army was considered next door to *lese-majeste*.

Lady Dorchester burnt all her husband's private papers after his death in 1808; so we have lost some of the most intimate records concerning him. But 'grave Carleton' appears so frequently in the letters of his friend Wolfe that we can see his character as a young man in almost any aspect short of self-revelation. The first reference has nothing to do with affairs of state. In 1747 Wolfe, aged twenty, writing to Miss Lacey, an English girl in Brussels, and signing himself 'most sincerely your friend and admirer, ' says: 'I was doing the greatest injustice to the dear girls to admit the least doubt of their constancy. Perhaps with respect to ourselves there may be cause of complaint. Carleton, I'm afraid, is a recent example of it. ' From this we may infer that Carleton was less 'grave' as a young man than Wolfe found him later on. Six years afterwards Wolfe strongly recommended him for a position which he had himself been asked to fill, that of military tutor to the young Duke of Richmond, who was to get a company in Wolfe's own regiment. Writing home from Paris in 1753 Wolfe tells his mother that the duke 'wants some skilful man to travel with him through the Low Countries and into Lorraine. I have proposed my friend Carleton, whom Lord Albemarle approves of. ' Lord Albemarle was the British ambassador to France; so Carleton got the post and travelled under the happiest auspices, while learning the frontier on which the Belgian, French, and British allies were to fight the Germans in the Great World War of 1914. It was during this military tour of fortified places that Carleton acquired the engineering skill which a few years later proved of such service to the British cause in Canada.

In 1754 George Washington, at that time a young Virginian officer of only twenty-two, fired the first shot in what presently became the world-wide Seven Years' War. The immediate result was disastrous to the British arms; and Washington had to give up the command of the Ohio by surrendering Fort Necessity to the French on—of all dates—the 4th of July! In 1755 came Braddock's defeat. In 1756 Montcalm arrived in Canada and won his first victory at Oswego. In 1757 Wolfe distinguished himself by formulating the plan which, if properly executed, would have prevented the British fiasco at Rochefort on the coast of France. But Carleton remained as undistinguished as before. He simply became lieutenant-colonel commanding the 72nd Foot, now the Seaforth Highlanders. In 1758 his chance appeared to have come at last. Amherst had asked for his services at Louisbourg. But the king had neither forgotten nor forgiven the remarks about the Hanoverians, and so refused point-blank, to Wolfe's 'very great grief and disappointment... It is a public loss Carleton's not going. ' Wolfe's confidence in Carleton, either as a friend or as an officer, was stronger than ever. Writing to George Warde, afterwards the famous cavalry leader, he said: 'Accidents may happen in the family that may throw my little affairs into disorder. Carleton is so good as to say he will give what help is in his power. May I ask the same favour of you, my oldest friend? ' Writing to Lord George Sackville, of whom we shall hear more than enough at the crisis of Carleton's career Wolfe said: 'Amherst will tell you his opinion of Carleton, by which you will probably be better convinced of our loss. ' Again, 'We want grave Carleton for every purpose of the war. ' And yet again, after the fall of Louisbourg: 'If His Majesty had thought proper to let Carleton come with us as engineer it would have cut the matter much shorter and we might now be ruining the walls of Quebec and completing the conquest of New France. ' A little later on Wolfe blazes out with indignation over Carleton's supersession by a junior. 'Can Sir John Ligonier (the commander-in-chief) allow His Majesty to remain unacquainted with the merit of that officer, and can he see such a mark of displeasure without endeavouring to soften or clear the matter up a little? A man of honour has the right to expect the protection of his Colonel and of the Commander of the troops, and he can't serve without it. If I was in Carleton's place I wouldn't stay an hour in the Army after being aimed at and distinguished in so remarkable a manner. ' But Carleton bided his time.

At the beginning of 1759 Wolfe was appointed to command the army destined to besiege Quebec. He immediately submitted Carleton's name for appointment as quartermaster-general. Pitt and Ligonier heartily approved. But the king again refused. Ligonier went back a second time to no purpose. Pitt then sent him in for the third time, saying, in a tone meant for the king to overhear: 'Tell His Majesty that in order to render the General [Wolfe] completely responsible for his conduct he should be made, as far as possible, inexcusable if he should fail; and that whatever an officer entrusted with such a service of confidence requests ought therefore to be granted. ' The king then consented. Thus began Carleton's long, devoted, and successful service for Canada, the Empire, and the Crown.

Early in this memorable Empire Year of 1759 he sailed with Wolfe and Saunders from Spithead. On the 30th of April the fleet rendezvoused at Halifax, where Admiral Durell, second-in-command to Saunders, had spent the winter with a squadron intended to block the St Lawrence directly navigation opened in the spring. Durell was a good commonplace officer, but very slow. He had lost many hands from sickness during a particularly cold season, and he was not enterprising enough to start cruising round Cabot Strait before the month of May. Saunders, greatly annoyed by this delay, sent him off with eight men-of-war on the 5th of May. Wolfe gave him seven hundred soldiers under Carleton. These forces were sufficient to turn back, capture, or destroy the twenty-three French merchantmen which were then bound for Quebec with supplies and soldiers as reinforcements for Montcalm. But the French ships were a week ahead of Durell; and, when he landed Carleton at Isle-aux-Coudres on the 28th of May, the last of the enemy's transports had already discharged her cargo at Quebec, sixty miles above.

Isle-aux-Coudres, so named by Jacques Cartier in 1535, was a point of great strategic importance; for it commanded the only channel then used. It was the place Wolfe had chosen for his winter quarters, that is, in case of failure before Quebec and supposing he was not recalled. None but a particularly good officer would have been appointed as its first commandant. Carleton spent many busy days here preparing an advanced base for the coming siege, while the subsequently famous Captain Cook was equally busy 'a-sounding of the channell of the Traverse' which the fleet would have to pass on its way to Quebec. Some of Durell's ships destroyed the French 'long-shore batteries near this Traverse, at the lower end of the island of Orleans, while the rest kept ceaseless watch to seaward, anxiously scanning the offing, day after day, to make out the colours of the first fleet up. No one knew what the French West India fleet would do; and there was a very disconcerting chance that it might run north and slip into the St Lawrence, ahead of Saunders, in the same way as the French reinforcements had just slipped in ahead of Durell. Presently, at the first streak of dawn on the 23rd of June, a strong squadron was seen advancing rapidly under a press of sail. Instantly the officers of the watch called all hands up from below. The boatswains' whistles shrilled across the water as the seamen ran to quarters and cleared the decks for action. Carleton's camp was equally astir. The guards turned out. The bugles sounded. The men fell in and waited. Then the flag-ship signalled ashore that the strangers had just answered correctly in private code that all was well and that Wolfe and Saunders were aboard.

Next to Wolfe himself Carleton was the busiest man in the army throughout the siege of Quebec. In addition to his arduous and very responsible duties as quartermaster-general, he acted as inspector of engineers and as a special-service officer for work of an exceptionally confidential nature. As quartermaster-general he superintended the supply and transport branches. Considering that the army was operating in a devastated hostile country, a thousand miles away from its bases at Halifax and Louisbourg, and that the interaction of the different services—naval and military, Imperial and Colonial—

required adjustment to a nicety at every turn, it was wonderful that so much was done so well with means which were far from being adequate. War prices of course ruled in the British camp. But they compared very favourably with the famine prices in Quebec, where most 'luxuries' soon became unobtainable at any price. There were no canteen or camp-follower scandals under Carleton. Then, as now, every soldier had a regulation ration of food and a regulation allowance for his service kit. But 'extras' were always acceptable. The price-list of these 'extras' reads strangely to modern ears. But, under the circumstances, it was not exorbitant, and it was slightly tempered by being reckoned in Halifax currency of four dollars to the pound instead of five. The British Tommy Atkins of that and many a later day thought Canada a wonderful country for making money go a long way when he could buy a pot of beer for twopence and get back thirteen pence Halifax currency as change for his English shilling. Beef and ham ran from ninepence to a shilling a pound. Mutton was a little dearer. Salt butter was eightpence to one-and-threepence. Cheese was tenpence; potatoes from five to ten shillings a bushel. 'A reasonable loaf of good soft Bread' cost sixpence. Soap was a shilling a pound. Tea was prohibitive for all but the officers. 'Plain Green Tea and very Badd' was fifteen shillings, 'Couchon' twenty shillings, 'Hyson' thirty. Leaf tobacco was tenpence a pound, roll one-and-tenpence, snuff two-and-threepence. Sugar was a shilling to eighteen pence. Lemons were sixpence apiece. The non-intoxicating 'Bad Sproos Beer' was only twopence a quart and helped to keep off scurvy. Real beer, like wine and spirits, was more expensive. 'Bristol Beer' was eighteen shillings a dozen, 'Bad malt Drink from Hellifax' ninepence a quart. Rum and claret were eight shillings a gallon each, port and Madeira ten and twelve respectively. The term 'Bad' did not then mean noxious, but only inferior. It stood against every low-grade article in the price-list. No goods were over-classified while Carleton was quartermaster-general.

The engineers were under-staffed, under-manned, and overworked. There were no Royal Engineers as a permanent and comprehensive corps till the time of Wellington. Wolfe complained bitterly and often of the lack of men and materials for scientific siege work. But he 'relied on Carleton' to good purpose in this respect as well as in many others. In his celebrated dispatch to Pitt he mentions Carleton twice. It was Carleton whom he sent to seize the west end of the island of Orleans, so as to command the basin of Quebec, and Carleton whom he sent to take prisoners and gather information at Pointe-aux-Trembles, twenty miles above the city. Whether or not he revealed the whole of his final plan to Carleton is probably more than we shall ever know, since Carleton's papers were destroyed. But we do know that he did not reveal it to any one else, not even to his three brigadiers, Monckton, Townshend, and Murray.

Carleton was wounded in the head during the Battle of the Plains; but soon returned to duty. Wolfe showed his confidence in him to the last. Carleton's was the only name mentioned twice in the will which Wolfe handed over to Jervis, the future Lord St Vincent, the night before the battle. 'I leave to Colonel Oughton, Colonel Carleton, Colonel Howe, and Colonel Warde a thousand pounds each. ' 'All my books and papers, both here and in England, I leave to Colonel Carleton. ' Wolfe's mother, who died five years later, showed the same confidence by appointing Carleton her executor.

With the fall of Quebec in 1759 Carleton disappears from the Canadian scene till 1766. But so many pregnant events happened in Canada during these seven years, while so few happened in his own career, that it is much more important for us to follow her history than his biography.

In 1761 he was wounded at the storming of Port Andro during the attack on Belle Isle off the west coast of France. In 1762 he was wounded at Havana in the West Indies. After that he enjoyed four years of quietness at home. Then came the exceedingly difficult task of guiding Canada through twelve years of turbulent politics and most subversive war.

CHAPTER II

GENERAL MURRAY 1759-1766

Both armies spent a terrible winter after the Battle of the Plains. There was better shelter for the French in Montreal than for the British among the ruins of Quebec. But in the matter of food the positions were reversed. Nevertheless the French gallantly refused the truce offered them by Murray, who had now succeeded Wolfe. They were determined to make a supreme effort to regain Quebec in the spring; and they were equally determined that the habitants should not be free to supply the British with provisions.

In spite of the state of war, however, the French and British officers, even as prisoners and captors, began to make friends. They had found each other foemen worthy of their steel. A distinguished French officer, the Comte de Malartic, writing to Levis, Montcalm's successor, said: 'I cannot speak too highly of General Murray, although he is our enemy. ' Murray, on his part, was equally loud and generous in his praise of the French. The Canadian seigneurs found fellow-gentlemen among the British officers. The priests and nuns of Quebec found many fellow-Catholics among the Scottish and Irish troops, and nothing but courteous treatment from the soldiers of every rank and form of religion. Murray directed that 'the compliment of the hat' should be paid to all religious processions. The Ursuline nuns knitted long stockings for the bare-legged Highlanders when the winter came on, and presented each Scottish officer with an embroidered St Andrew's Cross on the 30th of November, St Andrew's Day. The whole garrison won the regard of the town by giving up part of their rations for the hungry poor; while the habitants from the surrounding country presently began to find out that the British were honest to deal with and most humane, though sternly just, as conquerors.

In the following April Levis made his desperate throw for victory; and actually did succeed in defeating Murray outside the walls of Quebec. But the British fleet came up in May; and that summer three British armies converged on Montreal, where the last doomed remnants of French power on the St Lawrence stood despairingly at bay. When Levis found his two thousand effective French regulars surrounded by eight times as many British troops he had no choice but to lay down the arms of France for ever. On the 8th of September

1760 his gallant little army was included in the Capitulation of Montreal, by which the whole of Canada passed into the possession of the British Crown.

Great Britain had a different general idea for each one of the four decades which immediately followed the conquest of Canada. In the sixties the general idea was to kill refractory old French ways with a double dose of new British liberty and kindness, so that Canada might gradually become the loyal fourteenth colony of the Empire in America. But the fates were against this benevolent scheme. The French Canadians were firmly wedded to their old ways of life, except in so far as the new liberty enabled them to throw off irksome duties and restraints, while the new English-speaking 'colonists' were so few, and mostly so bad, that they became the cause of endless discord where harmony was essential. In the seventies the idea was to restore the old French-Canadian life so as not only to make Canada proof against the disaffection of the Thirteen Colonies but also to make her a safe base of operations against rebellious Americans. In the eighties the great concern of the government was to make a harmonious whole out of two very widely differing parts—the long-settled French Canadians and the newly arrived United Empire Loyalists. In the nineties each of these parts was set to work out its own salvation under its own provincial constitution.

Carleton's is the only personality which links together all four decades—the would-be American sixties, the French-Canadian seventies, the Anglo-French-Canadian eighties, and the bi-constitutional nineties—though, as mentioned already, Murray ruled Canada for the first seven years, 1759-66.

James Murray, the first British governor of Canada, was a younger son of the fourth Lord Elibank. He was just over forty, warm-hearted and warm-tempered, an excellent French scholar, and every inch a soldier. He had been a witness for the defence of Mordaunt at the court-martial held to try the authors of the Rochefort fiasco in 1757. Wolfe, who was a witness on the other side, referred to him later on as 'my old antagonist Murray. ' But Wolfe knew a good man when he saw one and gave his full confidence to his 'old antagonist' both at Louisbourg and Quebec. Murray was not born under a lucky star. He saw three defeats in three successive wars. He began his service with the abortive attack on pestilential Cartagena, where Wolfe's father was present as adjutant-general. In mid-career he lost the battle of Ste Foy. [Footnote: See *The Winning of Canada*, chap. viii. See also, for the best account of this battle and other events of the year between Wolfe's victory and the surrender of Montreal, *The Fall of Canada*, by George M. Wrong. Oxford, 1914.] And his active military life ended with his surrender of Minorca in 1782. But he was greatly distinguished for honour and steadfastness on all occasions. An admiring contemporary described him as a model of all the military virtues except prudence. But he had more prudence and less genius than his admirer thought; and he showed a marked talent for general government. The problem before him was harder than his superiors could believe. He was expected to prepare for assimilation some sixty-five thousand 'new subjects' who were mostly alien in religion and wholly alien in every other way. But, for the moment, this proved the least of his many difficulties because no immediate results were required.

While the war went on in Europe Canada remained nominally a part of the enemy's dominions, and so, of course, was subject to military rule. Sir Jeffery Amherst, the British commander-in-chief in America, took up his headquarters in New York. Under him Murray commanded Canada from Quebec. Under Murray, Colonel Burton commanded the district of Three Rivers while General Gage commanded the district of Montreal, which then extended to the western wilds. [Footnote: See *The War Chief of the Ottawas*, chap. iii.]

Murray's first great trouble arose in 1761. It was caused by an outrageous War Office order that fourpence a day should be stopped from the soldiers to pay for the rations they had always got free. Such gross injustice, coming in time of war and applied to soldiers who richly deserved reward, made the veterans 'mad with rage. ' Quebec promised to be the scene of a wild mutiny. Murray, like all his officers, thought the stoppage nothing short of robbery. But he threw himself into the breach. He assembled the officers and explained that they must die to the last man rather than allow the mutineers a free hand. He then held a general parade at which he ordered the troops to march between two flag-poles on pain of instant death, promising to kill with his own hands the first man who refused. He added that he was ready to hear and forward any well-founded complaint, but that, since insubordination had been openly threatened, he would insist on subordination being publicly shown. Then, amid tense silence, he gave the word of command— *Quick, March!* —while every officer felt his trigger. To the immense relief of all concerned the men stepped off, marched straight between the flags and back to quarters, tamed. The criminal War Office blunder was rectified and peace was restored in the ranks.

'Murray's Report' of 1762 gives us a good view of the Canada of that day and shows the attitude of the British towards their new possession. Canada had been conquered by Great Britain, with some help from the American colonies, for three main reasons: first, to strike a death-blow at French dominion in America; secondly, to increase the opportunities of British seaborne trade; and, thirdly, to enlarge the area available for British settlement. When Murray was instructed to prepare a report on Canada he had to keep all this in mind; for the government wished to satisfy the public both at home and in the colonies. He had to examine the military strength of the country and the disposition of its population in case of future wars with France. He had to satisfy the natural curiosity of men like the London merchants. And he had to show how and where English-speaking settlers could go in and make Canada not only a British possession but the fourteenth British colony in North America. Burton and Gage were also instructed to report about their own districts of Three Rivers and Montreal. The documents they prepared were tacked on to Murray's. By June 1762 the work was completed and sent on to Amherst, who sent it to England in ample time to be studied there before the opening of the impending negotiations for peace.

Murray was greatly concerned about the military strength of Quebec, then, as always, the key of Canada. Like the unfortunate Montcalm he found the walls of Quebec badly built, badly placed, and falling into ruins, and he thought they could not be defended by three thousand men against 'a well conducted *Coup-de-main*. ' He proposed to crown Cape Diamond with a proper citadel, which would overawe the disaffected in Quebec itself and defend the place against an outside enemy long enough to let a British fleet come up to its relief. The rest of the country was defended by little garrisons at Three Rivers and Montreal as well as by several small detachments distributed among the trading-posts where the white men and the red met in the depths of the western wilderness.

The relations between the British garrison and the French Canadians were so excellent that what Gage reported from Montreal might be taken as equally true of the rest of the country: 'The Soldiers live peaceably with the Inhabitants and they reciprocally acquire an affection for each other. ' The French Canadians numbered sixty-five thousand altogether, exclusive of the fur traders and coureurs de bois. Barely fifteen thousand lived in the three little towns of Quebec, Montreal, and Three Rivers; while over fifty thousand lived in the country. Nearly all the officials had gone back to France. The three classes of greatest importance were the seigneurs, the clergy, and the habitants. The lawyers were not of much account; the petty commercial classes of less account still. The coureurs de bois and other fur traders formed an important link between the savage and the civilized life of the country.

Apart from furs the trade of Canada was contemptibly small in the eyes of men like the London merchants. But the opportunity of fostering all the fur trade that could be carried down the St Lawrence was very well worth while; and if there was no other existing trade worth capturing there seemed to be some kinds worth creating. Murray held out well-grounded hopes of the fisheries and forests. 'A Most immense Cod Fishery can be established in the River and Gulph of St Lawrence. A rich tract of country on the South Side of the Gulph will be settled and improved, and a port or ports furnished with every material requisite to repair ships. ' He then went on to enumerate the other kinds of fishery, the abundance of whales, seals, and walruses in the Gulf, and of salmon up all the tributary rivers. Burton recommends immediate attention to the iron mines behind Three Rivers. All the governors expatiate on the vast amount of forest wealth and remind the home government that under the French regime the king, when making out patents for the seigneurs, reserved the right of taking wood for ship-building and fortifications from any of the seigneuries. Agriculture was found to be in a very backward state. The habitants would raise no more than they required for their own use and for a little local trade. But the fault was attributed to the gambling attractions of the fur trade, to the bad governmental system, and to the frequent interruptions of the *corvee*, a kind of forced labour which was meant to serve the public interest, but which Bigot and other thievish officials always turned to their own private advantage. On the whole, the reports were most encouraging in the prospects they held out to honest labour, trade, and government.

While Murray and his lieutenants had been collecting information for their reports the home government had been undergoing many changes for the worse. The master-statesman Pitt had gone out of power and the back-stairs politician Bute had come in. Pitt's 'bloody and expensive war'—the war that more than any other, laid the foundations of the present British Empire—was to be ended on any terms the country could be persuaded to bear. Thus the end of the Seven Years' War, or, as the British part of it was more correctly called, the 'Maritime War, ' was no more glorious in statesmanship than its beginning had been in arms. But the spirit of its mighty heart still lived on in the Empire's grateful memories of Pitt and quickened the English-speaking world enough to prevent any really disgraceful surrender of the hard-won fruits of victory.

The Treaty of Paris, signed on the 10th of February 1763, and the king's proclamation, published in October, were duly followed by the inauguration of civil government in Canada. The incompetent Bute, anxious to get Pitt out of the way, tried to induce him to become the first British governor of the new colony. Even Bute probably never dared to hope that Pitt would actually go out to Canada. But he did hope to lower his prestige by making him the holder of a sinecure at home. However this may be, Pitt, mightiest of all parliamentary ministers of war, refused to be made either a jobber or an exile; whereupon Murray's position was changed from a military command into that of 'Governor and Captain-General. '

The changes which ensued in the laws of Canada were heartily welcomed so far as the adoption of the humaner criminal code of England was concerned. The new laws relating to debtor and creditor also gave general satisfaction, except, as we shall presently see, when they involved imprisonment for debt. But the tentative efforts to introduce English civil law side by side with the old French code resulted in great confusion and much discontent. The land laws had become so unworkable under this dual system that they had to be left as they were. A Court of Common Pleas was set up specially for the benefit of the French Canadians. If either party demanded a jury one had to be sworn in; and French Canadians were to be jurors on equal terms with 'the King's Old Subjects. ' The Roman Catholic Church was to be completely tolerated but not in any way established. Lord Egremont, in giving the king's instructions to Murray, reminded him that the proviso in the Treaty of Paris—*as far as the Laws of Great Britain permit*—should govern his action whenever disputes arose. It must be remembered that the last Jacobite rising was then a comparatively recent affair, and that France was equally ready to upset either the Protestant succession in England or the British regime in Canada.

The Indians were also an object of special solicitude in the royal proclamation. 'The Indians who live under our Protection should not be molested in the possession of such parts of our Dominions and Territories as, not having been ceded to or purchased by Us, are reserved to them. ' The home government was far in advance of the American colonists in its humane attitude towards the Indians. The common American attitude then and long afterwards —indeed, up to a time well within living memory—was that Indians were a kind of human vermin to be exterminated without mercy, unless, of course, more money was to be made out of them alive. The result was an endless struggle along the ever-receding frontier of the West. And just at this particular time the 'Conspiracy of Pontiac' had brought about something like a real war. The story of this great effort of the Indians to stem the encroachments of the exterminating colonists is told in another chronicle of the present Series. [Footnote: The War Chief of the Ottawas.] The French traders in the West undoubtedly had a hand in stirring up the Indians. Pontiac, a sort of Indian Napoleon, was undoubtedly cruel as well as crafty. And the Indians undoubtedly fought just as the ancestors of the French and British used to fight when they were at the corresponding stage of social evolution. But the mere fact that so many jealously distinct tribes united in this common cause proves how much they all must have suffered at the hands of the colonists.

While Pontiac's war continued in the West Murray had to deal with a political war in Canada which rose to its height in 1764. The king's proclamation of the previous October had 'given express Power to our Governor that, so soon as the state and circumstances of the said Colony will admit thereof, he shall call a General Assembly in such manner and form as is used in those Colonies and Provinces in America which are under our immediate government. ' The intention of establishing parliamentary institutions was, therefore, perfectly clear. But it was equally clear that the introduction of such institutions was to depend on 'circumstances, ' and it is well to remember here that these 'circumstances' were not held to warrant the opening of a Canadian parliament till 1792. Now, the military government had been a great success. There was every reason to suppose that civil government by a governor and council would be the next best thing. And it was quite certain that calling a 'General Assembly' at once would defeat the very ends which such bodies are designed to serve. More than ninety-nine per cent of the population were dead against an assembly which none of them understood and all distrusted. On the other hand, the clamorous minority of less than one per cent were in favour only of a parliament from which the majority should be rigorously excluded, even, if possible, as voters. The immense majority comprised the entire French-Canadian community. The absurdly small minority consisted mostly of Americanized camp-following traders, who, having come to fish in troubled waters, naturally wanted the laws made to suit poachers. The British garrison, the governing officials, and the very few other English-speaking people of a more enlightened class all looked down on the rancorous minority. The whole question resolved itself into this: should Canada be handed over to the licensed exploitation of a few hundred low-class camp-followers, who had done nothing to win her for the British Empire, who were despised by those who had, and who promised to be a dangerous thorn in the side of the new colony?

What this ridiculous minority of grab-alls really wanted was not a parliament but a rump. Many a representative assembly has ended in a rump, The grab-alls wished to begin with one and stop there. It might be supposed that such pretensions would defeat themselves. But there was a twofold difficulty in the way of getting the truth understood by the English-speaking public on both sides of the Atlantic. In the first place, the French Canadians were practically dumb to the outside world. In the second, the vociferous rumpites had the ear of some English and more American commercial people who were not anxious to understand; while the great mass of the general public were inclined to think, if they ever thought at all, that parliamentary government must mean more liberty for every one concerned.

A singularly apt commentary on the pretensions of the camp-followers is supplied by the famous, or infamous, 'Presentment of the Grand Jury of Quebec' in October 1764. The moving spirits of this precious jury were aspirants to membership in the strictly exclusive, rumpish little parliament of their own seeking. The signatures of the French-Canadian members were obtained by fraud, as was subsequently proved by a sworn official protestation. The first presentment tells its own tale, as it refers to the only courts in which French-Canadian lawyers were allowed to plead. 'The great number of inferior Courts are tiresome, litigious, and expensive to this poor Colony. ' Then came a hit at the previous military rule—'That Decrees of the military Courts may be amended [after having been confirmed by legal ordinance] by allowing Appeals if the matter decided exceed Ten Pounds, ' which would put it out of the reach of the 'inferior Courts' and into the clutches of 'the King's Old Subjects. ' But the gist of it all was contained in the following: 'We represent that as the Grand Jury must be considered at present as the only Body representative of the Colony,... We propose that the Publick Accounts be laid before the Grand Jury at least twice a year. ' That the grand jury was to be purged of all its French-Canadian members is evident from the addendum slipped in behind their backs. This addendum is a fine specimen of verbose invective against 'the Church of Rome, ' the Pope, Bulls, Briefs, absolutions, etc., the empanelling 'en Grand and petty Jurys' of 'papist or popish Recusants Convict, ' and so on.

The 'Presentment of the Grand Jury' was presently followed by *The Humble Petition of Your Majesty's most faithful and loyal Subjects, British Merchants and Traders, in behalf of Themselves and their fellow Subjects, Inhabitants of Your Majesty's Province of Quebec.* 'Their fellow Subjects' did not, of course, include any 'papist or popish Recusants Convict. ' Among the 'Grievances and Distresses' enumerated were 'the oppressive and severely felt Military government, ' the inability to 'reap the fruit of our Industry' under such a martinet as Murray, who, in one paragraph, is accused of 'suppressing dutyfull Remonstrances in Silence' and, in the next, of 'treating them with a Rage and Rudeness of Language and Demeanor as dishonourable to the Trust he holds of Your Majesty as painfull to Those who suffer from it. ' Finally, the petitioners solemnly warn His Majesty that their 'Lives in the Province are so very unhappy that we must be under the Necessity of removing from it, unless timely prevented by a Removal of the present Governor. '

In forwarding this document Murray poured out the vials of his wrath on 'the Licentious Fanaticks Trading here, ' while he boldly championed the cause of the French Canadians, 'a Race, who, could they be indulged with a few priveledges which the Laws of England deny to Roman Catholicks at home, would soon get the better of every National Antipathy to their Conquerors and become the most faithful and most useful set of Men in this American Empire. '

While these charges and counter-charges were crossing the Atlantic another, and much more violent, trouble came to a head. As there were no barracks in Canada billeting was a necessity. It was made as little burdensome as possible and the houses of magistrates were specially exempt. This, however, did not prevent the magistrates from baiting the military whenever they got the chance. Fines, imprisonments, and other sentences, out of all proportion to the offence committed, were heaped on every redcoat in much the same way as was then being practised in Boston and other hotbeds of disaffection. The redcoats had done their work in ridding America of the old French menace. They were doing it now in ridding the colonies of the last serious menace from the Indians. And so the colonists, having no further use for them, began trying to make the land they had delivered too hot to hold them. There were, of course, exceptions; and the American colonists had some real as well as pretended grievances. But wantonly baiting the redcoats had already become a most discreditable general practice.

Montreal was most in touch with the disaffected people to the south. It also had a magistrate of the name of Walker, the most rancorous of all the disaffected magistrates in Canada. This Walker, well mated with an equally rancorous wife, was the same man who entertained Benjamin Franklin and the other commissioners sent by Congress into Canada in 1776, the year in which both the American Republic and a truly British Canada were born. He would not have been flattered could he have seen the entry Franklin made about him and his wife in a diary which is still extant. The gist of it was that wherever the Walkers might be they would soon set the place by the ears. Walker, of course, was foremost in the persecution of the redcoats; and he eagerly seized his opportunity when an officer was billeted in a house where a brother magistrate happened to be living as a lodger. Under such circumstances the magistrate could not claim exemption. But this made no difference either to him or to Walker. Captain Payne, the gentleman whose presence enraged these boors, was seized and thrown into gaol. The chief justice granted a writ of habeas corpus. But the mischief was done and resentment waxed high. The French-Canadian seigneurs sympathized with Payne, which added fuel to the magisterial flame; and Murray, scenting danger, summoned the whole bench down to Quebec.

But before this bench of bumbles started some masked men seized Walker in his own house and gave him a good sound thrashing. Unfortunately they spoilt the fair reprisal by cutting off his ear. That very night the news had run round Montreal and made a start for Boston and Quebec. Feeling ran high; and higher still when, a few weeks later, the civil magistrates vented their rage on several redcoats by imposing sentences exceeding even the utmost limits of their previous vindictive action. Montreal became panic-stricken lest the soldiers, baited past endurance, should break out in open violence. Murray drove up, post-haste, from Quebec, ordered the affected regiment to another station, reproved the offending magistrates, and re-established public confidence. Official and private rewards were offered to any witnesses who would identify Walker's assailants. But in vain. The smouldering fire burst out again under Carleton. But the mystery was never cleared up.

Things had now come to a crisis. The London merchants, knowing nothing about the internal affairs of Canada, backed the petition of the Quebec traders, who were quite unworthy of such support from men of real business probity and knowledge. The magisterial faction in Canada advertised their side of the case all over the colonies and in any sympathetic quarter they could find in England. The seigneurs sent home a warm defence of Murray; and Murray himself sent Cramahe, a very able Swiss officer in the British Army. The home government thus had plenty of contradictory evidence before it in 1765. The result was that Murray was called home in 1766, rather in a spirit of open-minded and sympathetic inquiry into his conduct than with any idea of censuring him. He never returned to Canada. But as he held the titular governorship for some time longer, and as he was afterwards employed in positions of great responsibility and trust, the verdict of the home authorities was clearly given in his favour.

The troublous year of 1764 saw another innovation almost as revolutionary, compared with the old regime, as the introduction of civil government itself. This was the issue of the first newspaper in Canada, where, indeed, it was also the first printed thing of any kind. Nova Scotia had produced an earlier paper, the *Halifax Gazette*, which lived an intermittent life from 1752 to 1800. But no press had ever been allowed in New France. The few documents that required printing had always been done in the mother country. Brown and Gilmore, two Philadelphians, were thus undertaking a pioneer business when they announced that 'Our Design is, in case we are fortunate enough to succeed, early in this spring to settle in this City [Quebec] in the capacity of Printers, and forthwith to publish a weekly newspaper in French and English. ' The *Quebec Gazette*, which first appeared on the 21st of the following June, has continued to the present time, though it is now a daily and is known as the *Quebec Chronicle*. Centenarian papers are not common in any country; and those that have lived over a century and a half are very few indeed. So the *Quebec Chronicle*, which is the second surviving senior in America, is also among the great press seniors of the world.

The original number is one of the curiosities of journalism. The publishers felt tolerably sure of having what was then considered a good deal of recent news for their three hundred readers during the open season. But, knowing that the supply would be both short and stale in winter, they held out prospects of a Canadian *Tatler* or *Spectator*, without, however, being rash enough to promise a supply of Addisons and Steeles. Their announcement makes curious reading at the present day.

The Rigour of Winter preventing the arrival of ships from *Europe*, and in a great measure interrupting the ordinary intercourse with the Southern Provinces, it will be necessary, in a paper designed for General Perusal, and Publick Utility, to provide some things of general Entertainment, independent of foreign intelligence: we shall therefore, on such occasions, present our Readers with such *Originals*, both in *Prose* and *Verse*, as will please the FANCY and instruct the JUDGMENT. And here we beg leave to observe that we shall have nothing so much at heart as the support of VIRTUE and MORALITY and the noble cause of LIBERTY. The refined amusements of LITERATURE, and the pleasing veins of well pointed wit, shall also be considered as necessary to this collection; interspersed with chosen pieces, and curious essays, extracted from the most celebrated authors; So that, blending PHILOSOPHY with POLITICKS, HISTORY, &c., the youth of both sexes will be improved and persons of all ranks agreeably and usefully entertained. And upon the whole we will labour to attain to all the exactness that so much variety will permit, and give as much variety as will consist with a reasonable exactness. And as this part of our project cannot be carried into execution without the correspondence of the INGENIOUS, we shall take all opportunities of acknowledging our obligations, to those who take the trouble of furnishing any matter which shall tend to entertainment or instruction. Our Intentions to please the *Whole*, without offence to any *Individual*, will be better evinced by our practice, than by writing volumes on the subject. This one thing we beg may be believed, that PARTY PREJUDICE, or PRIVATE SCANDAL, will never find a place in this PAPER.

CHAPTER III

GOVERNOR CARLETON 1766-1774

The twelve years of Carleton's first administration naturally fall into three distinct periods of equal length. During the first he was busily employed settling as many difficulties as he could, examining the general state of the country, and gradually growing into the change that was developing in the minds of the home government, the change, that is, from the Americanizing sixties to the French-Canadian seventies. During the second period he was in England, helping to shape the famous Quebec Act. During the third he was defending Canada from American attack and aiding the British counterstroke by every means in his power.

On the 22nd of September 1766 Carleton arrived at Quebec and began his thirty years' experience as a Canadian administrator by taking over the government from Colonel Irving, who had held it since Murray's departure in the spring. Irving had succeeded Murray simply because he happened to be the senior officer present at the time. Carleton himself was technically Murray's lieutenant till 1768. But neither of these facts really affected the course of Canadian history.

The Council, the magistrates, and the traders each presented. the new governor with an address containing the usual professions of loyal devotion. Carleton remarked in his dispatch that these separate addresses, and the marked absence of any united address, showed how much the population was divided. He also noted that a good many of the English-speaking minority had objected to the addresses on account of their own opposition to the Stamp Act, and that there had been some broken heads in consequence. Troubles enough soon engaged his anxious attention—troubles over the Indian trade, the rights and wrongs of the Canadian Jesuits, the wounded dignity of some members of the Council, and the still smouldering and ever mysterious Walker affair.

The strife between Canada and the Thirteen Colonies over the Indian trade of the West remained the same in principle as under the old regime. The Conquest had merely changed the old rivalry between two foreign powers into one between two widely differing British possessions; and this, because of the general unrest among the Americans, made the competition more bitter, if possible, than ever.

The Jesuits pressed their claims for recognition, for their original estates, and for compensation. But their order had fallen on evil days all over the world. It was not popular even in Canada. And the arrangement was that while the existing members were to be treated with every consideration the Society itself was to be allowed to die out.

The offended councillors went so far as to present Carleton with a remonstrance which Irving himself had the misfortune to sign. Carleton had consulted some members on points with which they were specially acquainted. The members who had not been consulted thereupon protested to Irving, who assured them that Carleton must have done so by accident, not design. But when Carleton received a joint letter in which they said, 'As you are pleased to signifye to Us by Coll. Irving that it was accident, & not Intention, ' he at once replied: 'As Lieutenant Colonel Irving has signified to you that the Part of my Conduct you think worthy of your Reprehension happened by Accident let him explain his reasons for so doing. He had no authority from me. ' Carleton then went on to say that he would consult any 'Men of Good Sense, Truth, Candour, and Impartial Justice' whenever he chose, no matter whether they were councillors or not.

The Walker affair, which now broke out again, was much more serious than the storm in the Council's teacup. It agitated the whole of Canada and threatened to range the population of Montreal and Quebec into two irreconcilable factions, the civil and the military. For the whole of the two years since Murray had been called upon to deal with it cleverly presented versions of Walker's views had been spread all over the colonies and worked into influential Opposition circles in England. The invectives against the redcoats and their friends the seigneurs were of the usual abusive type. But they had an unusually powerful effect at that particular time in the Thirteen Colonies as well as in what their authors hoped to make a Fourteenth Colony after a fashion of their own; and they looked plausible enough to mislead a good many moderate men in the mother country too. Walker's case was that he had an actual witness, as to the identity of his assailants, in the person of McGovoch, a discharged soldier, who laid information against one civilian, three British officers, and the celebrated French-Canadian leader, La Corne de St Luc. All the accused were arrested in their beds in Montreal and thrown into the common gaol. Walker objected to bail on the plea that his life would be in danger if they were allowed at large. He also sought to postpone the trial in order to punish the accused as much as possible, guilty or innocent. But William Hey, the chief justice, an able and upright man, would consent to postponement only on condition that bail should be allowed; so the trial proceeded. When the grand jury threw out the case against one of the prisoners Walker let loose such a flood of virulent abuse that moderate men were turned against him. In the end all the accused were honourably acquitted, while McGovoch, who was proved to have been a false witness from the first, was convicted of perjury. Carleton remained absolutely impartial all through, and even dismissed Colonel Irving and another member of the Council for heading a petition on behalf of the military prisoners.

The Walker affair was an instance of a bad case in which the law at last worked well. But there were many others in which it did not. What with the *Coutume de Paris*, which is still quoted in the province of Quebec; the other complexities of the old French law; the doubtful meanings drawn from the capitulation, the treaty, the proclamation, and the various ordinances; the instinctive opposition between the French Canadians and the English-speaking civilians; and, finally, what with the portents of subversive change that were already beginning to overshadow all America, —what with all this and more, Carleton found himself faced with a problem which no man could have solved to the satisfaction of every one concerned. Each side in a lawsuit took whatever amalgam of French and English codes was best for its own argument. But, generally speaking, the ingrained feeling of the French Canadians was against any change of their own laws that was not visibly and immediately beneficial to their own particular interests. Moreover, the use of the unknown English language, the worthlessness of the rapacious English-speaking magistrates, and the detested innovation of imprisonment for debt, all combined to make every part of English civil law hated simply because it happened to be English and not French. The home authorities were anxious to find some workable compromise. In 1767 Carleton exchanged several important dispatches with them; and in 1768 they sent out Maurice Morgan to study and report, after consultation with the chief justice and 'other well instructed persons. ' Morgan was an indefatigable and clear-sighted man who deserves to be gratefully remembered by both races; for he was a good friend both to the French Canadians before the Quebec Act and to the

United Empire Loyalists just before their great migration, when he was Carleton's secretary at New York. In 1769 the official correspondence entered the 'secret and confidential' stage with a dispatch from the home government to Carleton suggesting a House of Representatives to which, practically speaking, the towns would send Protestant members and the country districts Roman Catholics.

In 1770 Carleton sailed for England. He carried a good deal of hard-won experience with him, both on this point and on many others. He went home with a strong opinion not only against an assembly but against any immediate attempts at Anglicization in any form. The royal instructions that had accompanied his commission as 'Captain-General and Governor-in-chief' in 1768 contained directions for establishing the Church of England with a view to converting the whole population to its tenets later on. But no steps had been taken, and, needless to say, the French Canadians remained as Roman Catholic as ever.

An increasingly important question, soon to overshadow all others, was defence. In April 1768 Carleton had proposed the restoration of the seigneurial militia system. 'All the Lands here are held of His Majesty's Castle of St Lewis [the governor's official residence in Quebec]. The Oath which the Vassals [seigneurs] take is very Solemn and Binding. They are obliged to appear in Arms for the King's defence, in case his Province is attacked. ' Carleton pointed out that a hundred men of the Canadian seigneurial families were being kept on full pay in France, ready to return and raise the Canadians at the first opportunity. 'On the other hand, there are only about seventy of these officers in Canada who have been in the French service. Not one of them has been given a commission in the King's [George's] Service, nor is there One who, from any motive whatever, is induced to support His Government. ' The few French Canadians raised for Pontiac's war had of course been properly paid during the continuance of their active service. But they had been disbanded like mere militia afterwards, without either gratuities or half-pay for the officers. This naturally made the class from which officers were drawn think that no career was open to them under the Union Jack and turned their thoughts towards France, where their fellows were enjoying full pay without a break.

What made this the more serious was the weakness of the regular garrisons, all of which, put together, numbered only 1,627 men. Carleton calculated that about five hundred of 'the King's Old

Subjects' were capable of bearing arms; though most of them were better at talking than fighting. He had nothing but contempt for 'the flimsy wall round Montreal, ' and relied little more on the very defective works at Quebec. Thus with all his wonderful equanimity, 'grave Carleton' left Canada with no light heart when he took six months' leave of absence in 1770; and he would have been more anxious still if he could have foreseen that his absence was to be prolonged to no less than four years.

He had, however, two great satisfactions. He was represented at Quebec by a most steadfast lieutenant, the quiet, alert, discreet, and determined Cramahe; and he was leaving Canada after having given proof of a disinterestedness which was worthy of the elder Pitt himself. When Pitt became Paymaster-General of England he at once declined to use the two chief perquisites of his office, the interest on the government balance and the half per cent commission on foreign subsidies, though both were regarded as a kind of indirect salary. When Carleton became governor of Canada he at once issued a proclamation abolishing all the fees and perquisites attached to his position and explained his action to the home authorities in the following words: 'There is a certain appearance of dirt, a sort of meanness, in exacting fees on every occasion. I think it necessary for the King's service that his representative should be thought unsullied. ' Murray, who had accepted the fees, at first took umbrage. But Carleton soon put matters straight with him. The fact was that fees, and even certain perquisites, were no dishonour to receive, as they nearly always formed a recognized part, and often the whole, of a perfectly legal salary. But fees and perquisites could be abused; and they did lead to misunderstandings, even when they were not abused; while fixed salaries were free from both objections. So Carleton, surrounded by shamelessly rapacious magistrates and the whole vile camp-following gang, as well as by French Canadians who had suffered from the robberies of Bigot and his like, decided to sacrifice everything but his indispensable fixed salary in order that even the most malicious critics could not bring any accusation, however false, against the man who represented Britain and her king.

An interesting personal interlude, which was not without considerable effect on Canadian history, took place in the middle of Carleton's four years' stay in England. He was forty-eight and still a bachelor. Tradition whispers that these long years of single life were the result of a disappointing love affair with Jane Carleton, a pretty cousin, when both he and she were young. However that may be, he now proposed to Lady Anne Howard, whose father, the Earl of Effingham, was one of his greatest friends. But he was doomed to a second, though doubtless very minor, disappointment. Lady Anne, who probably looked on 'grave Carleton' as a sort of amiable, middle-aged uncle, had fallen in love with his nephew, whom she presently married, and with whom she afterwards went out to Canada, where her husband served under the rejected uncle himself. What added spice to this peculiar situation was the fact that Carleton actually married the younger sister of the too-youthful Lady Anne. When Lady Anne rejoined her sister and their bosom friend, Miss Seymour, after the disconcerting interview with Carleton, she explained her tears by saying they were due to her having been 'obliged to refuse the best man on earth. ' 'The more fool you! ' answered the younger sister, Lady Maria, then just eighteen, 'I only wish he had given me the chance! ' There, for the time, the matter ended. Carleton went back to his official duties in furtherance of the Quebec Act. His nephew and the elder sister made mutual love. Lady Maria held her tongue. But Miss Seymour had not forgotten; and one day she mustered up courage to tell Carleton the story of 'the more fool you! ' This decided him to act at once. He proposed; was accepted; and lived happily married for the rest of his long life. Lady Maria was small, fair-haired, and blue-eyed, which heightened her girlish appearance when, like Madame de Champlain, she came out to Canada with a husband more than old enough to be her father. But she had been brought up at Versailles. She knew all the aristocratic graces of the old regime. And her slight, upright figure— erect as any soldier's to her dying day—almost matched her husband's stalwart form in dignity of carriage.

The Quebec Act of 1774—the Magna Charta of the French-Canadian race—finally passed the House of Lords on the 18th of June. The general idea of the Act was to reverse the unsuccessful policy of ultimate assimilation with the other American colonies by making Canada a distinctly French-Canadian province. The Maritime Provinces, with a population of some thirty thousand, were to be as English as they chose. But a greatly enlarged Quebec, with a population of ninety thousand, and stretching far into the unsettled West, was to remain equally French-Canadian; though the rights of what it was then thought would be a perpetual English-speaking minority were to be safeguarded in every reasonable way. The whole country between the American colonies and the domains of the Hudson's Bay Company was included in this new Quebec, which comprised the southern half of what is now the Newfoundland Labrador, practically the whole of the modern provinces of Quebec and Ontario, and all the western lands between the Ohio and the Great Lakes as far as the Mississippi, that is, the modern American states of Ohio, Indiana, Illinois, Michigan, and Wisconsin.

The Act gave Canada the English criminal code. It recognized most of the French civil law, including the seigneurial tenure of land. Roman Catholics were given 'the free Exercise' of their religion, 'subject to the King's Supremacy' as defined 'by an Act made in the First Year of Queen Elizabeth, ' which Act, with a magnificently prophetic outlook on the future British Empire, was to apply to 'all the Dominions and Countries which then did, or thereafter should, belong to the Imperial Crown. ' The Roman Catholic clergy were authorized to collect 'their accustomed Dues and Rights' from members of their own communion. The new oath of allegiance to the Crown was silent about differences of religion, so that Roman Catholics might take it without question. The clergy and seigneurs were thus restored to an acknowledged leadership in church and state. Those who wanted a parliament were distinctly told that 'It is at present inexpedient to call an Assembly, ' and that a Council of from seventeen to twenty-three members, all appointed by the Crown, would attend to local government and have power to levy taxes for roads and public buildings only. Lands held 'in free and common socage' were to be dealt with by the laws of England, as was all property which could be freely willed away. A possible establishment of the Church of England was provided for but never put in operation.

In some ways the Act did, in other ways it did not, fulfil the objects of its framers. It was undoubtedly a generous concession to the leading French Canadians. It did help to keep Canada both British and Canadian. And it did open the way for what ought to have been a crushing attack on the American revolutionary forces. But it was not, and neither it nor any other Act could possibly have been, at that late hour, completely successful. It conciliated the seigneurs and the parochial clergy. But it did not, and it could not, also conciliate the lesser townsfolk and the habitants. For the last fourteen years the habitants had been gradually drifting away from their former habits of obedience and former obligations towards their leaders in church and state. The leaders had lost their old followers. The followers had found no new leaders of their own.

Naturally enough, there was great satisfaction among the seigneurs and the clergy, with a general feeling among government supporters, both in England and Canada, that the best solution of a very refractory problem had been found at last. On the other hand, the Opposition in England, nearly every one in the American colonies, and the great majority of English-speaking people in Newfoundland, the Maritime Provinces, and Canada itself were dead against the Act; while the habitants, resenting the privileges already reaffirmed in favour of the seigneurs and clergy, and suspicious of further changes in the same unwelcome direction, were neutral at the best and hostile at the worst.

The American colonists would have been angered in any case. But when they saw Canada proper made as unlike a 'fourteenth colony' as could be, and when they also saw the gates of the coveted western lands closed against them by the same detested Act—the last of the 'five intolerable acts' to which they most objected—their fury knew no bounds. They cursed the king, the pope, and the French Canadians with as much violence as any temporal or spiritual rulers had ever cursed heretics and rebels. The 'infamous and tyrannical ministry' in England was accused of 'contemptible subservience' to the 'bloodthirsty, idolatrous, and hypocritical creed' of the French Canadians. To think that people whose religion had spread 'murder, persecution, and revolt throughout the world' were to be entrenched along the St Lawrence was bad enough. But to see Crown protection given to the Indian lands which the Americans considered their own western 'birthright' was infinitely worse. Was the king of England to steal the valley of the Mississippi in the same way as the king of France?

It is easy to be wise after the event and hard to follow any counsel of perfection. But it must always be a subject of keen, if unavailing, regret that the French Canadians were not guaranteed their own way of life, within the limits of the modern province of Quebec, immediately after the capitulation of Montreal in 1760. They would then have entered the British Empire, as a whole people, on terms which they must all have understood to be exceedingly generous from any conquering power, and which they would have soon found out to be far better than anything they had experienced under the government of France. In return for such unexampled generosity they might have become convinced defenders of the only flag in the world under which they could possibly live as French Canadians. Their relations to each other, to the rest of a changing Canada, and to

26

the Empire would have followed the natural course of political evolution, with the burning questions of language, laws, and religion safely removed from general controversy in after years. The rights of the English-speaking minority could, of course, have been still better safeguarded under this system than under the distracting series of half-measures which took its place. There should have been no question of a parliament in the immediate future. Then, with the peopling of Ontario by the United Empire Loyalists and the growth of the Maritime Provinces on the other side, Quebec could have entered Carleton's proposed Confederation in the nineties to her own and every one else's best advantage.

On the other hand, the delay of fourteen years after the Capitulation of 1760 and the unwarrantable extension of the provincial boundaries were cardinal errors of the most disastrous kind. The delay, filled with a futile attempt at mistaken Americanization, bred doubts and dissensions not only between the two races but between the different kinds of French Canadians. When the hour of trial came disintegration had already gone too far. The mistake about the boundaries was equally bad. The western wilds ought to have been administered by a lieutenant-governor under the supervision of a governor-general. Even leasing them for a short term of years to the Hudson's Bay Company would have been better than annexing them to a preposterous province of Quebec. The American colonists would have doubtless objected to either alternative. But both could have been defended on sound principles of administration; while the sudden invasion of a new and inflated Quebec into the colonial hinterlands was little less than a declaration of war. The whole problem bristled with enormous difficulties, and the circumstances under which it had to be faced made an ideal solution impossible. But an earlier Quebec Act, without its outrageous boundary clause, would have been well worth the risk of passing; for the delay led many French Canadians to suppose, however falsely, that the Empire's need might always be their opportunity; and this idea, however repugnant to their best minds and better feelings, has persisted among their extreme particularists until the present day.

CHAPTER IV

INVASION 1775

Carleton's first eight years as governor of Canada were almost entirely occupied with civil administration. The next four were equally occupied with war; so much so, indeed, that the Quebec Act could not be put in force on the 1st of May 1775, as provided for in the Act itself, but only bit by bit much later on. There was one short session of the new Legislative Council, which opened on the 17th of August. But all men's minds were even then turned towards the Montreal frontier, whence the American invasion threatened to overspread the whole country and make this opening session the last that might ever be held. Most of the members were soon called away from the council-chamber to the field. No further session could be held either that year or the next; and Carleton was obliged to nominate the judges himself. The fifteen years of peace were over, and Canada had once more become an object of contention between two fiercely hostile forces.

The War of the American Revolution was a long and exceedingly complicated struggle; and its many varied fortunes naturally had a profound effect on those of Canada. But Canada was directly engaged in no more than the first three campaigns, when the Americans invaded her in 1775 and '76, and when the British used her as the base from which to invade the new American Republic in 1777. These first three campaigns formed a purely civil war within the British Empire. On each side stood three parties. Opponents were ranged against each other in the mother country, in the Thirteen Colonies, and in Canada. In the mother country the king and his party government were ranged against the Opposition and all who held radical or revolutionary views. Here the strife was merely political. But in the Thirteen Colonies the forces of the Crown were ranged against the forces of the new Continental Congress. The small minority of colonists who were afterwards known as the United Empire Loyalists sided with the Crown. A majority sided with the Congress. The rest kept as selfishly neutral as they could. Among the English-speaking civilians in Canada, many of whom were now of a much better class than the original camp-followers, the active loyalists comprised only the smaller half. The larger half sided with the Americans, as was only natural, seeing that most of them were immigrants from the Thirteen Colonies. But by no means all these sympathizers were ready for a fight. Among the French Canadians the loyalists included very few besides the seigneurs, the clergy, and a handful of educated people in Montreal, Three Rivers, and Quebec. The mass of the habitants were more or less neutral. But many of them were anti-British at first, while most of them were anti-American afterwards.

Events moved quickly in 1775. On the 19th of April the 'shot heard round the world' was fired at Lexington in Massachusetts. On the 1st of May, the day appointed for the inauguration of the Quebec Act, the statue of the king in Montreal was grossly defaced and hung with a cross, a necklace of potatoes, and a placard bearing the inscription, *Here's the Canadian Pope and English Fool—Voila le Pape du Canada et le sot Anglais*. Large rewards were offered for the detection of the culprits; but without avail. Excitement ran high and many an argument ended with a bloody nose.

Meanwhile three Americans were plotting an attack along the old line of Lake Champlain. Two of them were outlaws from the colony of New York, which was then disputing with the neighbouring colony of New Hampshire the possession of the lawless region in which all three had taken refuge and which afterwards became Vermont. Ethan Allen, the gigantic leader of the wild Green Mountain Boys, had a price on his head. Seth Warner, his assistant, was an outlaw of a somewhat humbler kind. Benedict Arnold, the third invader, came from Connecticut. He was a horse-dealer carrying on business with Quebec and Montreal as well as the West Indies. He was just thirty-four; an excellent rider, a dead shot, a very fair sailor, and captain of a crack militia company. Immediately after the affair at Lexington he had turned out his company, reinforced by undergraduates from Yale, had seized the New Haven powder magazine and marched over to Cambridge, where the Massachusetts Committeemen took such a fancy to him that they made him a colonel on the spot, with full authority to raise men for an immediate attack on Ticonderoga. The opportunity seemed too good to be lost; though the Continental Congress was not then in favour of attacking Canada, as its members hoped to see the Canadians throw off the yoke of empire on their own account. The British posts on Lake Champlain were absurdly undermanned. Ticonderoga contained two hundred cannon, but only forty men, none of whom expected an attack. Crown Point had only a sergeant and a dozen men to watch its hundred and thirteen pieces. Fort George, at the head of Lake George, was no better off; and nothing more had been done to man the fortifications at St Johns on the Richelieu, where there was an excellent sloop as well as many cannon in charge of the usual sergeant's guard. This want of preparation was no fault of Carleton's. He had frequently reported home on the need of more men. Now he had less than a thousand regulars to defend the whole country: and not another man was to arrive till the spring of next year. When Gage was hard pressed for reinforcements at Boston in the autumn of 1774 Carleton had immediately sent him two excellent battalions that could ill be spared from Canada. But when Carleton himself made a similar request, in the autumn of 1775, Admiral Graves, to his lasting dishonour, refused to sail up to Quebec so late as October.

The first moves of the three Americans smacked strongly of a well-staged extravaganza in which the smart Yankees never failed to score off the dunderheaded British. The Green Mountain Boys assembled on the east side of the lake. Spies walked in and out of Ticonderoga, exactly opposite, and reported to Ethan Allen that the commandant and his whole garrison of forty unsuspecting men would make an easy prey. Allen then sent eighty men down to Skenesborough (now Whitehall) at the southern end of the lake, to take the tiny post there and bring back boats for the crossing on the 10th of May. Then Arnold turned up with his colonel's commission, but without the four hundred men it authorized him to raise. Allen, however, had made himself a colonel too, with Warner as his second-in-command. So there were no less than three colonels for two hundred and thirty men. Arnold claimed the command by virtue of his Massachusetts commission. But the Green Mountain Boys declared they would follow no colonels but their own; and so Arnold, after being threatened with arrest, was appointed something like chief of the staff, on the understanding that he would make himself generally useful with the boats. This appointment was made at dawn on the 10th of May, just as the first eighty men were advancing to the attack after crossing over under cover of night. The British sentry's musket missed fire; whereupon he and the guard were rushed, while the rest of the garrison were surprised in their beds. Ethan Allen, who knew the fort thoroughly, hammered on the commandant's door and summoned him to surrender 'In the name of the Great Jehovah and the Continental Congress! ' The astonished commandant, seeing that resistance was impossible, put on his dressing-gown and paraded his disarmed garrison as prisoners of war. Seth Warner presently arrived with the rest of Allen's men and soon became the hero of Crown Point, which he took with the whole of its thirteen men and a hundred and thirteen cannon. Then Arnold had his own turn, in command of an expedition against the sergeant's guard, cannon, stores, fort, and sloop at St Johns on the Richelieu, all of which he captured in the same absurdly simple way. When he came sailing back the three victorious commanders paraded all their men and fired off many straggling fusillades of joy. In the meantime the Continental Congress at Philadelphia, with a delightful touch of unconscious humour, was gravely debating the following resolution, which was passed on the 1st of June: *That no Expedition or Incursion ought to be undertaken or made, by any Colony or body of Colonists, against or into Canada.*

The same Congress, however, found reasons enough for changing its mind before the month of May was out. The British forces in Canada had already begun to move towards the threatened frontier. They had occupied and strengthened St Johns. And the Americans were beginning to fear lest the command of Lake Champlain might again fall into British hands. On the 27th of May the Congress closed the phase of individual raids and inaugurated the phase of regular invasion by commissioning General Schuyler to 'pursue any measures in Canada that may have a tendency to promote the peace and security of these Colonies. ' Philip Schuyler was a distinguished member of the family whose head had formulated the 'Glorious Enterprize' of conquering New France in 1689. [Footnote: See, in this Series, *The Fighting Governor.*] So it was quite in line with the family tradition for him to be under orders to 'take possession of St Johns, Montreal, and any other parts of the country, ' provided always, adds the cautious Congress, that 'General Schuyler finds it practicable, and that it will not be disagreeable to the Canadians. '

A few days later Arnold was trying to get a colonelcy from the Convention of New York, whose members just then happened to be thinking of giving commissions to his rivals, the leaders of the Green Mountain Boys, while, to make the complication quite complete, these Boys themselves had every intention of electing officers on their own account. In the meantime Connecticut, determined not to be forestalled by either friend or foe, ordered a thousand men to Ticonderoga and commissioned a general called Wooster to command them. Thus early were sown the seeds of those dissensions between Congress troops and Colony troops which nearly drove Washington mad.

Schuyler reached Ticonderoga in mid-July and assumed his position as Congressional commander-in-chief. Unfortunately for the good of the service he had only a few hundred men with him; so Wooster, who had a thousand, thought himself the bigger general of the two. The Connecticut men followed Wooster's lead by jeering at Schuyler's men from New York; while the Vermonters added to the confusion by electing Seth Warner instead of Ethan Allen. In mid-August a second Congressional general arrived, making three generals and half a dozen colonels for less than fifteen hundred troops. This third general was Richard Montgomery, an ardent rebel of thirty-eight, who had been a captain in the British Army. He had sold his commission, bought an estate on the Hudson, and married a daughter of the Livingstons. The Livingstons headed the Anglo-American revolutionists in the colony of New York as the Schuylers headed the Knickerbocker Dutch. One of them was very active on the rebel side in Montreal and was soon to take the field at the head of the American 'patriots' in Canada. Montgomery was brother to the Captain Montgomery of the 43rd who was the only British officer to disgrace himself during Wolfe's Quebec campaign, which he did by murdering his French-Canadian prisoners at Chateau Richer because they had fought disguised as Indians. [Footnote: See *The Passing of New France*, p. 118.] Richard Montgomery was a much better man than his savage brother; though, as the sequel proves, he was by no means the perfect hero his American admirers would have the world believe. His great value at Ticonderoga was his professional knowledge and his ardour in the cause he had espoused. His presence 'changed the spirit of the camp. ' It sadly needed change. 'Such a set of pusillanimous wretches never were collected' is his own description in a despairing letter to his wife. The 'army, ' in fact, was all parts and no whole, and all the parts were mere untrained militia. Moreover, the spirit of the 'town meeting' ruled the camp. Even a battery could not be moved without consulting a council of war. Schuyler, though far more phlegmatic than Montgomery, agreed with him heartily about this and many other exasperating points. 'If Job had been a general in my situation, his memory had not been so famous for patience. '

Worn out by his worries, Schuyler fell ill and was sent to command the base at Albany. Montgomery then succeeded to the command of the force destined for the front. The plan of invasion approved by Washington was, first, to sweep the line of the Richelieu by taking St Johns and Chambly, then to take Montreal, next to secure the line of the St Lawrence, and finally to besiege Quebec. Montgomery's forces were to carry out all the preliminary parts alone. But Arnold was to join him at Quebec after advancing across country from the Kennebec to the Chaudiere with a flying column of Virginians and New Englanders.

Carleton opened the melancholy little session of the new Legislative Council at Quebec on the very day Montgomery arrived at Ticonderoga—the 17th of August. When he closed it, to take up the defence of Canada, the prospect was already black enough, though it grew blacker still as time went on. Immediately on hearing the news of Ticonderoga, Crown Point, and St Johns at the end of May he had sent every available man from Quebec to Montreal, whence Colonel Templer had already sent off a hundred and forty men to St Johns, while calling for volunteers to follow. The seigneurial class came forward at once. But all attempts to turn out the militia en masse proved utterly futile. Fourteen years of kindly British rule had loosened the old French bonds of government and the habitants were no longer united as part of one people with the seigneurs and the clergy. The rebels had been busy spreading insidious perversions of the belated Quebec Act, poisoning the minds of the habitants against the British government, and filling their imaginations with all sorts of terrifying doubts. The habitants were ignorant, credulous, and suspicious to the last degree. The most absurd stories obtained ready credence and ran like wildfire through the province. Seven thousand Russians were said to be coming up the St Lawrence— whether as friends or foes mattered nothing compared with the awful fact that they were all outlandish bogeys. Carleton was said to have a plan for burning alive every habitant he could lay his hands on. Montgomery's thousand were said to be five thousand, with many more to follow. And later on, when Arnold's men came up the Kennebec, it was satisfactorily explained to most of the habitants that it was no good resisting dead-shot riflemen who were bullet-proof themselves. Carleton issued proclamations. The seigneurs waved their swords. The clergy thundered from their pulpits. But all in vain. Two months after the American exploits on Lake Champlain Carleton gave a guinea to the sentry mounted in his honour by the local militia colonel, M. de Tonnancour, because this man was the first genuine habitant he had yet seen armed in the whole district of Three Rivers. What must Carleton have felt when the home government authorized him to raise six thousand of His Majesty's loyal French-Canadian subjects for immediate service and informed him that the arms and equipment for the first three thousand were already on the way to Canada! Seven years earlier it might still have been possible to raise French-Canadian counterparts of those Highland regiments which Wolfe had recommended and Pitt had so cordially approved. Carleton himself had recommended this excellent scheme at the proper time. But, though the home government even then agreed with him, they thought such a measure would raise more parliamentary and public clamour than they could safely face. The chance once lost was lost for ever.

Carleton had done what he could to keep the enemy at arm's length from Montreal by putting every available man into Chambly and St Johns. He knew nothing of Arnold's force till it actually reached Quebec in November. Quebec was thought secure for the time being, and so was left with a handful of men under Cramahe. Montreal had a few regulars and a hundred 'Royal Emigrants, ' mostly old Highlanders who had settled along the New York frontier after the Conquest. For the rest, it had many American and a few British sympathizers ready to fly at each others' throats and a good many neutrals ready to curry favour with the winners. Sorel was a mere post without any effective garrison. Chambly was held by only eighty men under Major Stopford. But its strong stone fort was well armed and quite proof against anything except siege artillery; while its little garrison consisted of good regulars who were well provisioned for a siege. The mass of Carleton's little force was at St Johns under Major Preston, who had 500 men of the 7th and 26th (Royal Fusiliers and Cameronians), 80 gunners, and 120 volunteers, mostly French-Canadian gentlemen. Preston was an excellent officer, and his seven hundred men were able to give a very good account of themselves as soldiers. But the fort was not nearly so strong as the one at Chambly; it had no natural advantages of position; and it was short of both stores and provisions.

The three successive steps for Montgomery to take were St Johns, Chambly, and Montreal. But the natural order of events was completely upset by that headstrong Yankee, Ethan Allen, who would have his private war at Montreal, and by that contemptible British officer, Major Stopford, who would not defend Chambly. Montgomery laid siege to St Johns on the 18th of September, but made no substantial progress for more than a month. He probably had no use for Allen at anything like a regular siege. So Allen and a Major Brown went on to 'preach politicks' and concert a rising with men like Livingston and Walker. Livingston, as we have seen already, belonged to a leading New York family which was very active in the rebel cause; and Livingston, Walker, Allen, and Brown would have made a dangerous anti-British combination if they could only have worked together. But they could not. Livingston hurried off to join Montgomery with four hundred 'patriots' who served their cause fairly well till the invasion was over. Walker had no military qualities whatever. So Allen and Brown were left to their own disunited devices. Montreal seemed an easy prey. It had plenty of rebel sympathizers. Nearly all the surrounding habitants were either neutrals or inclined to side with the Americans, though not as fighting men. Carleton's order to bring in all the ladders, so as to prevent an escalade of the walls, had met with general opposition and evasion. Nothing seemed wanting but a good working plan.

Brown, or possibly Allen himself, then hit upon the idea of treating Montreal very much as Allen had treated Ticonderoga. In any case Allen jumped at it. He jumped so far, indeed, that he forestalled Brown, who failed to appear at the critical moment. Thus, on the 24th of September, Allen found himself alone at Long Point with a hundred and twenty men in face of three times as many under the redoubtable Major Carden, a skilled veteran who had won Wolfe's admiration years before. Carden's force included thirty regulars, two hundred and forty militiamen, and some Indians, probably not over a hundred strong. The militia were mostly of the seigneurial class with a following of habitants and townsmen of both French and British blood. Carden broke Allen's flanks rounded up his centre, and won the little action easily, though at the expense of his own most useful life. Allen was very indignant at being handcuffed and marched off like a common prisoner after having made himself a colonel twice over. But Carleton had no respect for self-commissioned officers and had no soldiers to spare for guarding dangerous rebels. So he shipped Allen off to England, where that eccentric warrior was confined in Pendennis Castle near Falmouth in Cornwall.

This affair, small as it was, revived British hopes in Montreal and induced a few more militiamen and Indians to come forward. But within a month more was lost at Chambly than had been gained at Montreal. On the 18th of October a small American detachment attacked Chambly with two little field-guns and induced it to surrender on the 20th. If ever an officer deserved to be shot it was Major Stopford, who tamely surrendered his well-armed and well-provided fort to an insignificant force, after a flimsy resistance of only thirty-six hours, without even taking the trouble to throw his stores into the river that flowed beside his strong stone walls. The news of this disgraceful surrender, diligently spread by rebel sympathizers, frightened the Indians away from St Johns, thus depriving Major Preston, the commandant, of his best couriers at the very worst time. But the evil did not stop there; for nearly all the few French-Canadian militiamen whom the more distant seigneurs had been able to get under arms deserted *en masse*, with many threats against any one who should try to turn them out again.

Chambly is only a short day's march from Montreal to the west and St Johns to the south; so its capture meant that St Johns was entirely cut off from the Richelieu to the north and dangerously exposed to being cut off from Montreal as well. Its ample stores and munitions of war were a priceless boon to Montgomery, who now redoubled his efforts to take St Johns. But Preston held out bravely for the remainder of the month, while Carleton did his best to help him. A fortnight earlier Carleton had arrested that firebrand, Walker, who had previously refused to leave the country, though Carleton had given him the chance of doing so. Mrs Walker, as much a rebel as her husband, interviewed Carleton and noted in her diary that he 'said many severe Things in very soft & Polite Termes. ' Carleton was firm. Walker's actions, words, and correspondence all proved him a dangerous rebel whom no governor could possibly leave at large without breaking his oath of office. Walker, who had himself caused so many outrageous arrests, now not only resisted the legal arrest of his own person, but fired on the little party of soldiers who had been sent to bring him into Montreal. The soldiers then began to burn him out; whereupon he carried his wife to a window from which the soldiers rescued her. He then surrendered and was brought into Montreal, where the sight of him as a prisoner made a considerable impression on the waverers.

A few hundred neighbouring militiamen were scraped together. Every one of the handful of regulars who could be spared was turned out. And Carleton set off to the relief of St Johns. But Seth Warner's Green Mountain Boys, reinforced by many more sharpshooters, prevented Carleton from landing at Longueuil, opposite Montreal. The remaining Indians began to slink away. The French-Canadian militiamen deserted fast—'thirty or forty of a night. ' There were not two hundred regulars available for a march across country. And on the 30th Carleton was forced to give up in despair. Within the week St Johns surrendered with 688 men, who were taken south as prisoners of war. Preston had been completely cut off and threatened with starvation as well. So when he destroyed everything likely to be needed by the enemy he had done all that could be expected of a brave and capable commander.

It was the 3rd of November when St Johns surrendered. Ten days later Montgomery occupied Montreal and Arnold landed at Wolfe's Cove just above Quebec. The race for the possession of Quebec had been a very close one. The race for the capture of Carleton was to be closer still. And on the fate of either depended the immediate, and perhaps the ultimate, fate of Canada.

The race for Quebec had been none the less desperate because the British had not known of the danger from the south till after Arnold had suddenly emerged from the wilds of Maine and was well on his way to the mouth of the Chaudiere, which falls into the St Lawrence seven miles above the city. Arnold's subsequent change of sides earned him the execration of the Americans. But there can be no doubt whatever that if he had got through in time to capture Quebec he would have become a national hero of the United States. He had the advantage of leading picked men; though nearly three hundred faint-hearts did turn back half-way. But, even with picked men, his feat was one of surpassing excellence. His force went in eleven hundred strong. It came out, reduced by desertion as well as by almost incredible hardships, with barely seven hundred. It began its toilsome ascent of the Kennebec towards the end of September, carrying six weeks' supplies in the bad, hastily built boats or on the men's backs. Daniel Morgan and his Virginian riflemen led the way. Aaron Burr was present as a young volunteer. The portages were many and trying. The settlements were few at first and then wanting altogether. Early in October the drenched portagers were already sleeping in their frozen clothes. The boats began to break up. Quantities of provisions were lost. Soon there was scarcely anything left but flour and salt pork. It took nearly a fortnight to get past the Great Carrying Place, in sight of Mount Bigelow. Rock, bog, and freezing slime told on the men, some of whom began to fall sick. Then came the chain of ponds leading into Dead River. Then the last climb up to the height-of-land beyond which lay the headwaters of the Chaudiere, which takes its rise in Lake Megantic.

There were sixty miles to go beyond the lake, and a badly broken sixty miles they were, before the first settlement of French Canadians could be reached. There was no trail. Provisions were almost at an end. Sickness increased. The sick began to die. 'And what was it all for? A chance to get killed! The end of the march was Quebec —

impregnable! ' On the 24th of October Arnold, with fifteen other men, began 'a race against time, a race against starvation' by pushing on ahead in a desperate effort to find food. Within a week he had reached the first settlement, after losing three of his five boats with everything in them. Three days later, and not one day too soon, the French Canadians met his seven hundred famishing men with a drove of cattle and plenty of provisions. The rest of the way was toilsome enough. But it seemed easy by comparison. The habitants were friendly, but very shy about enlisting, in spite of Washington's invitation to 'range yourselves under the standard of general liberty. ' The Indians were more responsive, and nearly fifty joined on their own terms. By the 8th of November Arnold was marching down the south shore of the St Lawrence, from the Chaudiere to Point Levis, in full view of Quebec. He had just received a dispatch ten days old from Montgomery by which he learned that St Johns was expected to fall immediately and that Schuyler was no longer with the army at the front. But he could not tell when the junction of forces would be made; and he saw at once that Quebec was on the alert because every boat had been either destroyed or taken over to the other side.

The spring and summer had been anxious times enough in Quebec. But the autumn was a great deal worse. Bad news kept coming down from Montreal. The disaffected got more and more restless and began 'to act as though no opposition might be shown the rebel forces. ' And in October it did seem as if nothing could be done to stop the invaders. There were only a few hundred militiamen that could be depended on. The regulars, under Colonel Maclean, had gone up to help Carleton on the Montreal frontier. The fortifications were in no state to stand a siege. But Cramahe was full of steadfast energy. He had mustered the French-Canadian militia on September 11, the very day Arnold was leaving Cambridge in Massachusetts for his daring march against Quebec. These men had answered the call far better in the city of Quebec than anywhere else. There was also a larger proportion of English-speaking loyalists here than in Montreal. But no transports brought troops up the St Lawrence from Boston or the mother country, and no vessel brought Carleton down. The loyalists were, however, encouraged by the presence of two small men-of-war, one of which, the *Hunter*, had been the guide-ship for Wolfe's boat the night before the Battle of the Plains. Some minor reinforcements also kept arriving: veterans from the border settlements and a hundred and fifty men from Newfoundland. On the 3rd of November, the day St Johns surrendered to Montgomery, an intercepted dispatch had warned Cramahe of Arnold's approach and led him to seize all the boats on the south shore opposite Quebec. This was by no means his first precaution. He had sent some men forty miles up the Chaudiere as soon as the news of the raids on Lake Champlain and St Johns had arrived at the end of May. Thus, though neither of them had anticipated such a bolt from the blue, both Carleton and Cramahe had taken all the reasonable means within their most restricted power to provide against unforeseen contingencies.

Arnold's chance of surprising Quebec had been lost ten days before he was able to cross the St Lawrence; and when the habitants on the south shore were helping his men to make scaling-ladders the British garrison on the north had already become too strong for him. But he was indefatigable in collecting boats and canoes at the mouth of the Chaudiere, and at other points higher up than Cramahe's men had reached when on their mission of destruction or removal, and he was as capable as ever when, on the pitch-black night of the 13th, he led his little flotilla through the gap between the two British men-of-war, the *Hunter* and the *Lizard*. The next day he marched across the Plains of Abraham and saluted Quebec with three cheers. But meanwhile Colonel Maclean, who had set out to help Carleton at Montreal and turned back on hearing the news of St Johns, had slipped into Quebec on the 12th. So Arnold found himself with less than seven hundred effectives against the eleven hundred British who were now behind the walls. After vainly summoning the city to surrender he retired to Pointe-aux-Trembles, more than twenty miles up the north shore of the St Lawrence, there to await the arrival of the victorious Montgomery.

Meanwhile Montgomery was racing for Carleton and Carleton was racing for Quebec. Montgomery's advance-guard had hurried on to Sorel, at the mouth of the Richelieu, forty-five miles below Montreal, to mount guns that would command the narrow channel through which the fugitive governor would have to pass on his way to Quebec. They had ample time to set the trap; for an incessant nor'-easter blew up the St Lawrence day after day and held Carleton fast in Montreal, while, only a league away, Montgomery's main body was preparing to cross over. Escape by land was impossible, as the Americans held Berthier, on the north shore, and had won over the habitants, all the way down from Montreal, on both sides of the river. At last, on the afternoon of the 11th, the wind shifted. Immediately a single cannon-shot was fired, a bugle sounded the *fall in!* and 'the whole military establishment' of Montreal formed up in the barrack square—one hundred and thirty officers and men, all told. Carleton, 'wrung to the soul, ' as one of his officers wrote home, came on parade 'firm, unshaken, and serene. ' The little column then marched down to the boats through shuttered streets of timid neutrals and scowling rebels. The few loyalists who came to say good-bye to Carleton at the wharf might well have thought it was the last handshake they would ever get from a British 'Captain-General and Governor-in-chief' as they saw him step aboard in the dreary dusk of that November afternoon. And if he and they had known the worst they might well have thought their fate was sealed; for neither of them then knew that both sides of the St Lawrence were occupied in force at two different places on the perilous way to Quebec.

The little flotilla of eleven vessels got safely down to within a few miles of Sorel, when one grounded and delayed the rest till the wind failed altogether at noon on the 12th. The next three days it blew upstream without a break. No progress could be made as there was no room to tack in the narrow passages opposite Sorel. On the third day an American floating battery suddenly appeared, firing hard. Behind it came a boat with a flag of truce and the following summons from Colonel Easton, who commanded Montgomery's advance-guard at Sorel:

> SIR, —By this you will learn that General Montgomery is in Possession of the Fortress Montreal. You are very sensible that I am in Possession at this Place, and that, from the strength of the United Colonies on both sides your own situation is Rendered Very disagreeable. I am therefore induced to make you the following Proposal, viz. :—That if you will Resign your Fleet to me Immediately, without destroying the Effects on Board, You and Your men shall be used with due civility, together with women & Children on Board. To this I shall expect Your direct and Immediate answer. Should you Neglect You will Cherefully take the Consequences which will follow.

Carleton was surprised: and well he might be. He had not supposed that Montgomery's men were in any such commanding position. But, like Cramahe at Quebec, he refused to answer; whereupon Easton's batteries opened both from the south shore and from Isle St Ignace. Carleton's heaviest gun was a 9-pounder; while Easton had four 12-pounders, one of them mounted on a rowing battery that soon forced the British to retreat. The skipper of the schooner containing the powder magazine wanted to surrender on the spot, especially when he heard that the Americans were getting some hot shot ready for him. But Carleton retreated upstream, twelve miles above Sorel, to Lavaltrie, just above Berthier on the north shore, where, on attempting to land, he was driven back by some Americans and habitants. Next morning, the 16th, a fateful day for Canada, the same Major Brown who had failed Ethan Allen at Montreal came up with a flag of truce to propose that Carleton should send an officer to see for himself how well all chance of escape had now been cut off. The offer was accepted; and Brown explained the situation from the rebel point of view. 'This is my small battery; and, even if you should chance to escape, I have a grand battery at the mouth of the Sorel [Richelieu] which will infallibly sink all of your vessels. Wait a little till you see the 32-pounders that are now within half-a-mile. ' There was a good deal of Yankee bluff in this warning, especially as the 32-pounders could not be mounted in time. But the British officer seemed perfectly satisfied that the way was completely blocked; and so the Americans felt sure that Carleton would surrender the following day.

Carleton, however, was not the man to give in till the very last; and one desperate chance still remained. His flotilla was doomed. But he might still get through alone without it. One of the French-Canadian skippers, better known as 'Le Tourte' or 'Wild Pigeon' than by his own name of Bouchette because of his wonderfully quick trips, was persuaded to make the dash for freedom. So Carleton, having ordered Prescott, his second-in-command, not to surrender the flotilla before the last possible moment, arranged for his own escape in a whaleboat. It was with infinite precaution that he made his preparations, as the enemy, though confident of taking him, were still on the alert to prevent such a prize from slipping through their fingers. He dressed like a habitant from head to foot, putting on a tasselled *bonnet rouge* and an *etoffe du pays* (grey homespun) suit of clothes, with a red sash and *bottes sauvages* like Indian moccasins. Then the whaleboat was quietly brought alongside. The crew got in and plied their muffled oars noiselessly down to the narrow passage between Isle St Ignace and the Isle du Pas, where they shipped the oars and leaned over the side to paddle past the nearest battery with the palms of their hands. It was a moment of breathless excitement; for the hope of Canada was in their keeping and no turning back was possible. But the American sentries saw no furtive French Canadians gliding through that dark November night and heard no suspicious noises above the regular ripple of the eddying island current. One tense half-hour and all was over, The oars were run out again; the men gave way with a will; and Three Rivers was safely reached in the morning.

Here Carleton met Captain Napier, who took him aboard the armed ship *Fell*, in which he continued his journey to Quebec. He was practically safe aboard the *Fell*; for Arnold had neither an army strong enough to take Quebec nor any craft big enough to fight a ship. But the flotilla above Sorel was doomed. After throwing all its powder into the St Lawrence it surrendered on the 19th, the very day Carleton reached Quebec. The astonished Americans were furious when they found that Carleton had slipped through their fingers after all. They got Prescott, whom they hated; and they released Walker, whom Carleton was taking as a prisoner to Quebec. But no friends and foes like Walker and Prescott could make up for the loss of Carleton, who was the heart as well as the head of Canada at bay.

The exultation of the British more than matched the disappointment of the Americans. Thomas Ainslie, collector of customs and captain of militia at Quebec, only expressed the feelings of all his fellow-loyalists when he made the following entry in the extremely accurate diary he kept throughout those troublous times:

'On the 19th (a Happy Day for Quebec!), to the unspeakable joy of the friends of the Government, and to the utter Dismay of the abettors of Sedition and Rebellion, General Carleton arrived in the *Fell*, arm'd ship, accompanied by an arm'd schooner. We saw our Salvation in his Presence. '

CHAPTER V

BELEAGUERMENT 1775-1776

When Carleton finally turned at bay within the walls of Quebec the British flag waved over less than a single one out of the more than a million square miles that had so recently been included within the boundaries of Canada. The landward walls cut off the last half-mile of the tilted promontory which rises three hundred feet above the St Lawrence but only one hundred above the valley of the St Charles. This promontory is just a thousand yards wide where the landward walls run across it, and not much wider across the world-famous Heights and Plains of Abraham, which then covered the first two miles beyond. The whole position makes one of Nature's strongholds when the enemy can be kept at arm's length. But Carleton had no men to spare for more than the actual walls and the narrow little strip of the Lower Town between the base of the cliff and the St Lawrence. So the enemy closed in along the Heights' and among the suburbs, besides occupying any point of vantage they chose across the St Lawrence or St Charles.

The walls were by no means fit to stand a siege, a fact which Carleton had frequently reported. But, as the Americans had neither the men nor the material for a regular siege, they were obliged to confine themselves to a mere beleaguerment, with the chance of taking Quebec by assault. One of Carleton's first acts was to proclaim that every able-bodied man refusing to bear arms was to leave the town within four days. But, though this had the desired effect of clearing out nearly all the dangerous rebels, the Americans still believed they had enough sympathizers inside to turn the scale of victory if they could only manage to take the Lower Town, with all its commercial property and shipping, or gain a footing anywhere within the walls.

There were five thousand souls left in Quebec, which was well provisioned for the winter. The women, children, and men unfit to bear arms numbered three thousand. The 'exempts' amounted to a hundred and eighty. As there was a growing suspicion about many of these last, Carleton paraded them for medical examination at the beginning of March, when, a good deal more than half were found quite fit for duty. These men had been malingering all winter in order to skulk out of danger; so he treated them with extreme leniency in only putting them on duty as a 'company of Invalids. ' But the slur stuck fast. The only other exceptions to the general efficiency were a very few instances of cowardice and many more of slackness. The militia order-books have repeated entries about men who turned up late for even important duties as well as about others whose authorized substitutes were no better than themselves. But it should be remembered that, as a whole, the garrison did exceedingly good service and that all the malingerers and serious delinquents together did not amount to more than a tenth of its total, which is a small proportion for such a mixed body.

The effective strength at the beginning of the siege was eighteen hundred of all ranks. Only one hundred of these belonged to the regular British garrison in Canada — a few staff-officers, twenty-two men of the Royal Artillery, and seventy men of the 7th Royal Fusiliers, a regiment which was to be commanded in Quebec sixteen years later by Queen Victoria's father, the Duke of Kent. The Fusiliers and two hundred and thirty 'Royal Emigrants' were formed into a little battalion under Colonel Maclean, a first-rate officer and Carleton's right-hand man in action. 'His Majesty's Royal Highland Regiment of Emigrants, ' which subsequently became the 84th Foot, now known as the 2nd York and Lancaster, was hastily raised in 1775 from the Highland veterans who had settled in the American colonies after the Peace of 1763. Maclean's two hundred and thirty were the first men he could get together in time to reach Quebec. The only other professional fighters were four hundred blue-jackets and thirty-five marines of H. M.SS. *Lizard* and *Hunter*, who were formed into a naval battalion under their own officers, Captains Hamilton and McKenzie, Hamilton being made a lieutenant-colonel and McKenzie a major while doing duty ashore. Fifty masters and mates of trading vessels were enrolled in the same battalion. The whole of the shipping was laid up for the winter in the Cul de Sac, which alone made the Lower Town a prize worth taking. The 'British Militia' mustered three hundred and thirty, the 'Canadian Militia' five hundred and forty-three. These two corps included practically all the official and business classes in Quebec and formed nearly half the total combatants. Some of them took no pay and were not bound to service beyond the neighbourhood of Quebec, thus being very much like the Home Guards raised all over Canada and the rest of the Empire during the Great World War of 1914. All the militia wore dark green coats with buff waistcoats and breeches. The total of eighteen hundred was completed by a hundred and twenty 'artificers, ' that is, men who would now belong to the Engineers,

Ordnance, and Army Service Corps. As the composition of this garrison has been so often misrepresented, it may be as well to state distinctly that the past or present regulars of all kinds, soldiers and sailors together, numbered eight hundred and the militia and other non-regulars a thousand. The French Canadians, very few of whom were or had been regulars, formed less than a third of the whole.

Montgomery and Arnold had about the same total number of men. Sometimes there were more, sometimes less. But what made the real difference, and what really turned the scale, was that the Americans had hardly any regulars and that their effectives rarely averaged three-quarters of their total strength. The balance was also against them in the matter of armament. For, though Morgan's Virginians had many more rifles than were to be found among the British, the Americans in general were not so well off for bayonets and not so well able to use those they had; while the artillery odds were still more against them. Carleton's artillery was not of the best. But it was better than that of the Americans. He decidedly overmatched them in the combined strength of all kinds of ordnance—cannons, carronades, howitzers, mortars, and swivels. Cannons and howitzers fired shot and shell at any range up to the limit then reached, between two and three miles. Carronades were on the principle of a gigantic shotgun, firing masses of bullets with great effect at very short ranges—less than that of a long musket-shot, then reckoned at two hundred yards. The biggest mortars threw 13-inch 224-lb shells to a great distance. But their main use was for high-angle fire, such as that from the suburb of St Roch under the walls of Quebec. Swivels were the smallest kind of ordnance, firing one-, two-, or three-pound balls at short or medium ranges. They were used at convenient points to stop rushes, much like modern machine-guns.

Thanks chiefly to Cramahe, the defences were not nearly so 'ruinous' as Arnold at first had thought them. The walls, however useless against the best siege artillery, were formidable enough against irregular troops and makeshift batteries; while the warehouses and shipping in the Lower Town were protected by two stockades, one straight under Cape Diamond, the other at the corner where the Lower Town turns into the valley of the St Charles. The first was called the Pres-de-Ville, the second the Sault-au-Matelot. The shipping was open to bombardment from the Levis shore. But the Americans had no guns to spare for this till April.

Montgomery's advance was greatly aided by the little flotilla which Easton had captured at Sorel. Montgomery met Arnold at Pointe-aux-Trembles, twenty miles above Quebec, on the 2nd of December and supplied his little half-clad force with the British uniforms taken at St Johns and Chambly. He was greatly pleased with the magnificent physique of Arnold's men, the fittest of an originally well-picked lot. He still had some 'pusillanimous wretches' among his own New Yorkers, who resented the air of superiority affected by Arnold's New Englanders and Morgan's Virginians. He felt a well-deserved confidence in Livingston and some of the English-speaking Canadian 'patriots' whom Livingston had brought into his camp before St Johns in September. But he began to feel more and more doubtful about the French Canadians, most of whom began to feel more and more doubtful about themselves. On the 6th he arrived before Quebec and took up his quarters in Holland House, two miles beyond the walls, at the far end of the Plains of Abraham. The same day he sent Carleton the following summons:

SIR; —Notwithstanding the personal ill-treatment I have received at your hands—notwithstanding your cruelty to the unhappy Prisoners you have taken, the feelings of humanity induce me to have recourse to this expedient to save you from the Destruction which hangs over you. Give me leave, Sir, to assure you that I am well acquainted with your situation. A great extent of works, in their nature incapable of defence, manned with a motley crew of sailors, the greatest part our friends; of citizens, who wish to see us within their walls, & a few of the worst troops who ever stiled themselves Soldiers. The impossibility of relief, and the certain prospect of wanting every necessary of life, should your opponents confine their operations to a simple Blockade, point out the absurdity of resistance. Such is your situation! I am at the head of troops accustomed to Success, confident of the righteousness of the cause they are engaged in, inured to danger, & so highly incensed at your inhumanity, illiberal abuse, and the ungenerous means employed to prejudice them in the mind of the Canadians that it is with difficulty I restrain them till my Batteries are ready from assaulting your works, which afford them a fair opportunity of ample vengeance and just retaliation. Firing upon a flag of truce, hitherto unprecedented, even among savages, prevents my taking the ordinary mode of communicating my sentiments. However, I will at any rate acquit my conscience. Should you persist in an unwarrantable defence, the consequences be upon your own head. Beware of destroying stores of any kind, Publick or Private, as you have done at Montreal and in Three Rivers— If you do, by Heaven, there will be no mercy shown.

Though Montgomery wrote bunkum like the common politician of that and many a later age, he was really a brave soldier. What galled him into fury was 'grave Carleton's' quiet refusal to recognize either him or any other rebel commander as the accredited leader of a hostile army. It certainly must have been exasperating for the general of the Continental Congress to be reduced to such expedients as tying a grandiloquent ultimatum to an arrow and shooting it into the beleaguered town. The charge of firing on flags of truce was another instance of 'talking for Buncombe. ' Carleton never fired on any white flag. But he always sent the same answer: that he could hold no communication with any rebels unless they came to implore the king's pardon. This, of course, was an aggravation of his offensive calmness in the face of so much revolutionary rage. To individual rebels of all sorts he was, if anything, over-indulgent. He would not burn the suburbs of Quebec till the enemy forced him to it, though many of the houses that gave the Americans the best cover belonged to rebel Canadians. He went out of his way to be kind to all prisoners, especially if sick or wounded. And it was entirely owing to his restraining influence that the friendly Indians had not raided the border settlements of New England during the summer. Nor was he animated only by the very natural desire of bringing back rebellious subjects to what he thought their true allegiance, as his subsequent actions amply proved. He simply acted with the calm dignity and impartial justice which his position required.

Three days before Christmas the bombardment began in earnest. The non-combatants soon found, to their equal amazement and delight, that a good many shells did very little damage if fired about at random. But news intended to make their flesh creep came in at the same time, and probably had more effect than the shells on the weak-kneed members of the community. Seven hundred scaling-ladders, no quarter if Carleton persisted in holding out, and a prophecy attributed to Montgomery that he would eat his Christmas dinner either in Quebec or in Hell—these were some of the blood-curdling items that came in by petticoat or arrow post. One of the most active purveyors of all this bombast was Jerry Duggan, a Canadian 'patriot' barber now become a Continental major.

But there was a serious side. Deserters and prisoners, as well as British adherents who had escaped, all began to tell the same tale, though with many variations. Montgomery was evidently bent on storming the walls the first dark night. His own orders showed it.

HEAD QUARTERS, HOLLAND HOUSE.
Near Quebec, 15th Decr. 1755.

The General having in vain offered the most favourable terms of accommodation to the Governor of Quebec, & having taken every possible step to prevail on the inhabitants to desist from seconding him in his wild scheme of defending the Town—for the speedy reduction of the only hold possessed by the Ministerial Troops in this Province— The soldiers, flushed with continual success, confident of the justice of their cause, & relying on that Providence which has uniformly protected them, will advance with alacrity to the attack of works incapable of being defended by the wretched Garrison posted behind them, consisting of Sailors unacquainted with the use of arms, of Citizens incapable of Soldiers' duty, & of a few miserable Emigrants. The General is confident that a vigorous & spirited attack must be attended with success. The Troops shall have the effects of the Governor, Garrison, & of such as have been active in misleading the Inhabitants & distressing the friends of liberty, equally divided among them, except the 100th share out of the whole, which shall be at the disposal of the General to be given to such soldiers as distinguished themselves by their activity & bravery, to be sold at public auction: the whole to be conducted as soon as the City is in our hands and the inhabitants disarmed.

It was a week after these orders had been written before the first positive news of the threatened assault was brought into town by an escaped British prisoner who, strangely enough, bore the name of Wolfe. Wolfe's escape naturally caused a postponement of Montgomery's design and a further council of war. Unlike most councils of war this one was full of fight. Three feints were to be made at different points while the real attack was to be driven home at Cape Diamond. But just after this decision had been reached two rebel Montrealers came down and, in another debate, carried the day for another plan. These men, Antell and Price, were really responsible for the final plan, which, like its predecessor, did not meet with Montgomery's approval. Montgomery wanted to make a breach before trying the walls. But he was no more than the chairman of a committee; and this egregious committee first decided to storm the unbroken walls and then changed to an attack on the Lower Town only. Antell was Montgomery's engineer. Price was a red-hot agitator. Both were better at politics than soldiering. Their argument was that if the Lower Town could be taken the Quebec militia would force Carleton to surrender in order to save the warehouses, shipping, and other valuable property along the waterfront, and that even if Carleton held out in debate he would soon be brought to his knees by the Americans, who would march through the gates, which were to be opened by the 'patriots' inside.

Another week passed; and Montgomery had not eaten his Christmas dinner either in Quebec or in the other place. But both sides knew the crisis must be fast approaching; for the New Yorkers had sworn that they would not stay a minute later than the end of the year, when their term of enlistment was up. Thus every day that passed made an immediate assault more likely, as Montgomery had to strike before his own men left him. Yet New Year's Eve itself began without the sign of an alarm.

Carleton had been sleeping in his clothes at the Recollets', night after night, so that he might be first on parade at the general rendezvous on the Place d'Armes, which stood near the top of Mountain Hill, the only road between the Upper and the Lower Town. Officers and men off duty had been following his example; and every one was ready to turn out at a moment's notice.

A north-easterly snowstorm was blowing furiously, straight up the St Lawrence, making Quebec a partly seen blur to the nearest American patrols and the Heights of Abraham a wild sea of whirling drifts to the nearest British sentries. One o'clock passed, and nothing stirred. But when two o'clock struck at Holland House Montgomery rose and began to put the council's plan in operation. The Lower Town was to be attacked at both ends. The Pres-de-Ville barricade was to be carried by Montgomery and the Sault-au-Matelot by Arnold, while Livingston was to distract Carleton's attention as much as possible by making a feint against the landward walls, where the British still expected the real attack. Livingston's Canadian fighting 'patriots' waded through the drifts, against the storm, across the Plains, and took post close in on the far side of Cape Diamond, only eighty yards from the same walls that were to have been stormed some days before. Jerry Duggan's parasitic Canadian 'patriots' took post in the suburb of St John and thence round to Palace Gate. Montgomery led his own column straight to Wolfe's Cove, whence he marched in along the narrow path between the cliff and the St Lawrence till he reached the spot at the foot of Cape Diamond just under the right of Livingston's line. Arnold, whose quarters were in the valley of the St Charles, took post in St Roch, with a mortar battery to fire against the walls and a column of men to storm the Sault-au-Matelot. Livingston's and Jerry Duggan's whole command numbered about four hundred men, Montgomery's five hundred, Arnold's six. The opposing totals were fifteen hundred Americans against seventeen hundred British. There was considerable risk of confusion between friend and foe, as most of the Americans, especially Arnold's men, wore captured British uniforms with nothing to distinguish them but odds and ends of their former kits and a sort of paper hatband bearing the inscription *Liberty or Death*.

A little after four the sentries on the walls at Cape Diamond saw lights flashing about in front of them and were just going to call the guard when Captain Malcolm Fraser of the Royal Emigrants came by on his rounds and saw other lights being set out in regular order like lamps in a street. He instantly turned out the guards and pickets. The drums beat to arms. Every church bell in the city pealed forth its alarm into that wild night. The bugles blew. The men off duty swarmed on to the Place d'Armes, where Carleton, calm and intrepid as ever, took post with the general reserve and waited. There was nothing for him to do just yet. Everything that could have been foreseen had already been amply provided for; and in his quiet confidence his followers found their own.

Towards five o'clock two green rockets shot up from Montgomery's position beside the Anse des Meres under Cape Diamond. This was the signal for attack. Montgomery's column immediately struggled on again along the path leading round the foot of the Cape towards the Pres-de-Ville barricade. Livingston's serious 'patriots' on the top of the Cape changed their dropping shots into a hot fire against the walls; while Jerry Duggan's little mob of would-be looters shouted and blazed away from safer cover in the suburbs of St John and St Roch. Arnold's mortars pitched shells all over the town; while his storming-party advanced towards the Sault-au-Matelot barricade. Carleton, naturally anxious about the landward walls, sent some of the British militia to reinforce the men at Cape Diamond, which, as he knew, Montgomery considered the best point of attack. The walls lower down did not seem to be in any danger from Jerry Duggan's 'patriots, ' whose noisy demonstration was at once understood to be nothing but an empty feint. The walls facing the St Charles were well manned and well gunned by the naval battalion. Those facing the St Lawrence, though weak in themselves, were practically impregnable, as the cliffs could not be scaled by any formed body. The Lower Town, however, was by no means so safe, in spite of its two barricades. The general uproar was now so great that Carleton could not distinguish the firing there from what was going on elsewhere. But it was at these two points that the real attack was rapidly developing.

The first decisive action took place at Pres-de-Ville. The guard there consisted of fifty men—John Coffin, who was a merchant of Quebec, Sergeant Hugh McQuarters of the Royal Artillery, Captain Barnsfair, a merchant skipper, with fifteen mates and skippers like himself, and thirty French Canadians under Captain Chabot and Lieutenant Picard. These fifty men had to guard a front of only as many feet. On their right Cape Diamond rose almost sheer. On their left raged the stormy St Lawrence. They had a tiny block-house next to the cliff and four small guns on the barricade, all double-charged with canister and grape. They had heard the dropping shots on the top of the Cape for nearly an hour and had been quick to notice the change to a regular hot fire. But they had no idea whether their own post was to be attacked or not till they suddenly saw the head of Montgomery's column halting within fifty paces of them. A man came forward cautiously and looked at the barricade. The storm was in his face. The defences were wreathed in whirling snow. And the men inside kept silent as the grave. When he went back a little group stood for a couple of minutes in hurried consultation. Then Montgomery waved his sword, called out 'Come on, brave boys, Quebec is ours! ' and led the charge. The defenders let the Americans get about half-way before Barnsfair shouted 'Fire! ' Then the guns and muskets volleyed together, cutting down the whole front of the densely massed column. Montgomery, his two staff-officers, and his ten leading men were instantly killed. Some more farther back were wounded. And just as the fifty British fired their second round the rest of the five hundred Americans turned and ran in wild confusion.

A few minutes later a man whose identity was never established came running from the Lower Town to say that Arnold's men had taken the Sault-au-Matelot barricade. If this was true it meant that the Pres-de-Ville fifty would be caught between two fires. Some of them made as if to run back and reach Mountain Hill before the Americans could cut them off. But Coffin at once threatened to kill the first man to move; and by the time an artillery officer had arrived with reinforcements perfect order had been restored. This officer, finding he was not wanted there, sent back to know where else he was to go, and received an answer telling him to hurry to the Sault-au-Matelot. When he arrived there, less than half a mile off, he found that desperate street fighting had been going on for over an hour.

Arnold's advance had begun at the same time as Livingston's demonstration and Montgomery's attack. But his task was very different and the time required much longer. There were three obstacles to be overcome. First, his men had to run the gauntlet of the fire from the bluejackets ranged along the Grand Battery, which faced the St Charles at its mouth and overlooked the narrow little street of Sous-le-Cap at a height of fifty or sixty feet. Then they had to take the small advanced barricade, which stood a hundred yards on the St Charles side of the actual Sault-au-Matelot or Sailor's Leap, which is the north-easterly point of the Quebec promontory and nearly a hundred feet high. Finally, they had to round this point and attack the regular Sault-au-Matelot barricade. This second barricade was about a hundred yards long, from the rock to the river. It crossed Sault-au-Matelot Street and St Peter Street, which were the same then as now. But it ended on a wharf half-way down the modern St James Street, as the outer half of this street was then a natural strand completely covered at high tide. It was much closer than the Pres-de-Ville barricade was to Mountain Hill, at the top of which Carleton held his general reserve ready in the Place d'Armes; and it was fairly strong in material and armament. But it was at first defended by only a hundred men.

The American forlorn hope, under Captain Oswald, got past most of the Grand Battery unscathed. But by the time the main body was following under Morgan the British blue-jackets were firing down from the walls at less than point-blank range. The driving snow, the clumps of bushes on the cliff, and the little houses in the street below all gave the Americans some welcome cover. But many of them were hit; while the gun they were towing through the drifts on a sleigh stuck fast and had to be abandoned. Captain Dearborn, the future commander-in-chief of the American army in the War of 1812, noted in his diary that he 'met the wounded men very thick' as he was bringing up the rear. When the forlorn hope reached the advanced barricade Arnold halted it till the supports had come up. The loss of the gun and the worrying his main body was receiving from the sailors along the Grand Battery spoilt his original plan of smashing in the barricade by shell fire while Morgan circled round its outer flank on the ice of the tidal flats and took it in rear. So he decided on a frontal attack. When he thought he had a fair chance he stepped to the front and shouted, 'Now, boys, all together, rush! ' But before he could climb the barricade he was shot through the leg. For some time he propped himself up against a house and, leaning on his rifle, continued encouraging his men, who were soon firing through the port-holes as well as over the top. But presently growing faint from loss of blood he had to be carried off the field to the General Hospital on the banks of the St Charles.

The men now called out for a lead from Morgan, who climbed a ladder, leaped the top, and fell under a gun inside. In another minute the whole forlorn hope had followed him, while the main body came close behind. The guard, not strong in numbers and weak in being composed of young militiamen, gave way but kept on firing. 'Down with your arms if you want quarter! ' yelled Morgan, whose men were in overwhelming strength; and the guard surrendered. A little way beyond, just under the bluff of the Sault-au-Matelot, the British supports, many of whom were Seminary students, also surrendered to Morgan, who at once pressed on, round the corner of the Sault-au-Matelot, and halted in sight of the second or regular barricade. What was to be done now? Where was Montgomery? How strong was the barricade; and had it been reinforced? It could not be turned because the cliff rose sheer on one flank while the icy St Lawrence lashed the other. Had Morgan known that there were only a hundred men behind it when he attacked its advanced barricade he might have pressed on at all costs and carried it by assault. But it looked strong, there were guns on its platforms, and it ran across two streets. His hurried council of war over-ruled him, as Montgomery's council had over-ruled the original plan of storming the walls; and so his men began a desultory fight in the streets and from the houses.

This was fatal to American success. The original British hundred were rapidly reinforced. The artillery officer who had found that he was not needed at the Pres-de-Ville after Montgomery's defeat, and who had hurried across the intervening half-mile, now occupied the corner houses, enlarged the embrasures, and trained his guns on the houses occupied by the enemy. Detachments of Fusiliers and Royal

Emigrants also arrived, as did the thirty-five masters and mates of merchant vessels who were not on guard with Barnsfair at the Pres-de-Ville. Thus, what with soldiers, sailors, and militiamen of both races, the main Sault-au-Matelot barricade was made secure against being rushed like the outer one. But there was plenty of fighting, with some confusion at close quarters caused by the British uniforms which both sides were wearing. A Herculean sailor seized the first ladder the Americans set against the barricade, hauled it up, and set it against the window of a house out of the far end of which the enemy were firing. Major Nairne and Lieutenant Dambourges of the Royal Emigrants at once climbed in at the head of a storming-party and wild work followed with the bayonet. All the Americans inside were either killed or captured. Meanwhile a vigorous British nine-pounder had been turned on another house they occupied. This house was likewise battered in, so that its surviving occupants had to run into the street, where they were well plied with musketry by the regulars and militiamen. The chance for a sortie then seeming favourable, Lieutenant Anderson of the Navy headed his thirty-five merchant mates and skippers in a rush along Sault-au-Matelot Street. But his effort was premature. Morgan shot him dead, and Morgan's Virginians drove the seamen back inside the barricade.

Carleton had of course kept in perfect touch with every phase of the attack and defence; and now, fearing no surprise against the walls in the growing daylight, had decided on taking Arnold's men in rear. To do this he sent Captain Lawes of the Royal Engineers and Captain McDougall of the Royal Emigrants with a hundred and twenty men out through Palace Gate. This detachment had hardly reached the advanced barricade before they fell in with the enemy's rearguard, which they took by complete surprise and captured to a man. Leaving McDougall to secure these prisoners before following on, Lawes pushed eagerly forward, round the corner of the Sault-au-Matelot cliff, and, running in among the Americans facing the main barricade, called out, 'You are all my prisoners! ' 'No, we're not; you're ours! ' they answered. 'No, no, ' replied Lawes, as coolly as if on parade 'don't mistake yourselves, I vow to God you're mine! ' 'But where are your men? ' asked the astonished Americans; and then Lawes suddenly found that he was utterly alone! The roar of the storm and the work of securing the prisoners on the far side of the advanced barricade had prevented the men who should have followed him from understanding that only a few were needed with McDougall. But Lawes put a bold face on it and answered, 'O, Ho, make yourselves easy! My men are all round here and they'll be with you in a twinkling. ' He was then seized and disarmed. Some of the Americans called out, 'Kill him! Kill him! ' But a Major Meigs protected him. The whole parley had lasted about ten minutes when McDougall came running up with the missing men, released Lawes, and made prisoners of the nearest Americans. Lawes at once stepped forward and called on the rest to surrender. Morgan was for cutting his way through. A few men ran round by the wharf and escaped on the tidal flats of the St Charles. But, after a hurried consultation, the main body, including Morgan, laid down their arms. This was decisive. The British had won the fight.

The complete British loss in killed and wounded was wonderfully small, only thirty, just one-tenth of the corresponding American loss, which was large out of all proportion. Nearly half of the fifteen hundred Americans had gone—over four hundred prisoners and about three hundred killed and wounded. Nor were the mere numbers the most telling point about it; for the worse half escaped—Livingston's Montreal 'patriots, ' many of whom had done very little fighting, Montgomery's time-expired New Yorkers, most of whom wanted to go home, and Jerry Duggan's miscellaneous rabble, all of whom wanted a maximum of plunder with a minimum of war.

The British victory was as nearly perfect as could have been desired. It marked the turn of the tide in a desperate campaign which might have resulted in the total loss of Canada. And it was of the greatest significance and happiest augury because all the racial elements of this new and vast domain had here united for the first time in defence of that which was to be their common heritage. In Carleton's little garrison of regulars and militia, of bluejackets, marines, and merchant seamen, there were Frenchmen and French Canadians, there were Englishmen, Irishmen, Scotsmen, Welshmen, Orcadians, and Channel Islanders, there were a few Newfoundlanders, and there mere a good many of those steadfast Royal Emigrants who may be fitly called the forerunners of the United Empire Loyalists. Yet, in spite of this remarkable significance, no public memorial of Carleton has ever been set up; and it was only in the twentieth century that the Dominion first thought of commemorating his most pregnant victory by placing tablets to mark the sites of the two famous barricades.

As soon as things had quieted down within the walls Carleton sent out search-parties to bring in the dead for decent burial and to see if any of the wounded had been overlooked. James Thompson, the assistant engineer, saw a frozen hand protruding from a snowdrift at Pres-de-Ville. It was Montgomery's. The thirteen bodies were dug out and Thompson was ordered to have a 'genteel coffin made for Mr Montgomery, ' who was buried in the wall just above St Louis Gate by the Anglican chaplain. Thompson kept Montgomery's sword, which was given to the Livingston family more than a century later.

The beleaguerment continued, in a half-hearted way, till the spring. The Americans received various small reinforcements, which eventually brought their total up to what it had been under Montgomery's command. But there were no more assaults. Arnold grew dissatisfied and finally went to Montreal; while Wooster, the new general, who arrived on the 1st of April, was himself succeeded by Thomas, an ex-apothecary, on the 1st of May. The suburb of St Roch was burnt down after the victory; so the American snipers were bereft of some very favourite cover, and this, with other causes, kept the bulk of the besiegers at an ineffective distance from the walls.

The British garrison had certain little troubles of its own; for discipline always tends to become irksome after a great effort. Carleton was obliged to stop the retailing of spirits for fear the slacker men would be getting out of hand. The guards and duties were made as easy as possible, especially for the militia. But the 'snow-shovel parade' was an imperative necessity. The winter was very stormy, and the drifts would have frequently covered the walls and even the guns if they had not promptly been dug out. The cold was also unusually severe. One early morning in January an angry officer was asking a sentry why he hadn't challenged him, when the sentry said, 'God bless your Honour! and I'm glad you're come, for I'm blind! ' Then it was found that his eyelids were frozen fast together.

News came in occasionally from the outside world. There was intense indignation among the garrison when they learned that the American commanders in Montreal were imprisoning every Canadian officer who would not surrender his commission. Such an unheard-of outrage was worthy of Walker. But others must have thought of it; for Walker was now in Philadelphia giving all the evidence he could against Prescott and other British officers. Bad news for the rebels was naturally welcomed, especially anything about their growing failure to raise troops in Canada. On hearing of

Montgomery's defeat the Continental Congress had passed a resolution, addressed to the 'Inhabitants of Canada' declaring that 'we will never abandon you to the unrelenting fury of your and our enemies. ' But there were no trained soldiers to back this up; and the raw militia, though often filled with zeal and courage, could do nothing to redress the increasingly adverse balance. In the middle of March the Americans sent in a summons. But Carleton refused to receive it; and the garrison put a wooden horse and a bundle of hay on the walls with a placard bearing the inscription, 'When this horse has eaten this bunch of hay we will surrender. ' Some excellent practice made with 13-inch shells sent the Americans flying from their new battery at Levis; and by the 17th of March one of the several exultant British diarists, whose anonymity must have covered an Irish name, was able to record that 'this, being St Patrick's Day, the Governor, who is a true Hibernian, has requested the garrison to put off keeping it till the 17th of May, when he promises, they shall be enabled to do it properly, and with the usual solemnities. '

A fortnight later a plot concerted between the American prisoners and their friends outside was discovered just in time. With tools supplied by traitors they were to work their way out of their quarters, overpower the guard at the nearest gate, set fire to the nearest houses in three different streets, turn the nearest guns inwards on the town, and shout 'Liberty for ever! ' as an additional signal to the storming-party that was to be waiting to confirm their success. Carleton seized the chance of turning this scheme against the enemy. Three safe bonfires were set ablaze. The marked guns were turned inwards and fired at the town with blank charges. And the preconcerted shout was raised with a will. But the besiegers never stirred. After this the Old-Countrymen among the prisoners, who had taken the oath and enlisted in the garrison, were disarmed and confined, while the rest were more strictly watched.

Two brave attempts were made by French Canadians to reach Quebec with reinforcements, one headed by a seigneur, the other by a parish priest. Carleton had sent word to M. de Beaujeu, seigneur of Crane Island, forty miles below Quebec, asking him to see if he could cut off the American detachment on the Levis shore. De Beaujeu raised three hundred and fifty men. But Arnold sent over reinforcements. A habitant betrayed his fellow-countrymen's advance-guard. A dozen French Canadians were then killed or wounded while forty were taken prisoners; whereupon the rest dispersed to their homes. The other attempt was made by Father Bailly, whose little force of about fifty men was also betrayed. Entrapped in a country-house these men fought bravely till nearly half their number had been killed or wounded and the valiant priest had been mortally hit. They then surrendered to a much stronger force which had lost more men than they.

This was on the 6th of April, just before Arnold was leaving in disgust. Wooster made an effort to use his new artillery to advantage by converging the fire of three batteries, one close in on the Heights of Abraham, another from across the mouth of the St Charles, and the third from Levis. But the combination failed: the batteries were too light for the work and overmatched by the guns on the walls, the practice was bad, and the effect was nil. On the 3rd of May the new general, Thomas, an enterprising man, tried a fireship, which was meant to destroy all the shipping in the Cul de Sac. It came on, under full sail, in a very threatening manner. But the crew lost their nerve at the critical moment, took to the boats too soon, and forgot to lash the helm. The vessel immediately flew up into the wind and, as the tidal stream was already changing, began to drift away from the Cul de Sac just when she burst into flame. The result, as described by an enthusiastic British diarist, was that 'she affoard'd a very pritty prospect while she was floating down the River, every now & then sending up Sky rackets, firing of Cannon or bursting of Shells, & so continued till She disappear'd in the Channell. '

Three days later, on the 6th of May, when the beleaguerment had lasted precisely five months, the sound of distant gunfire came faintly up the St Lawrence with the first breath of the dawn wind from the east. The sentries listened to make sure; then called the sergeants of the guards, who sent word to the officers on duty, who, in their turn, sent word to Carleton. By this time there could be no mistake. The breeze was freshening; the sound was gradually nearing Quebec; and there could hardly be room for doubting that it came from the vanguard of the British fleet. The drums beat to arms, the church bells rang, the news flew round to every household in Quebec; and before the tops of the *Surprise* frigate were seen over the Point of Levy every battery was fully manned, every battalion was standing ready on the Grand Parade, and every non-combatant man, woman, and child was lining the seaward wall. The regulation shot was fired across her bows as she neared the city; whereupon she fired three guns to leeward, hoisted the private signal, and showed the Union Jack. Then, at last, a cheer went up that told both friend and foe of British victory and American defeat. By a strange coincidence the parole for this triumphal day was St George, while the parole appointed for the victorious New Year's Eve had been St Denis; so that the patron saints of France and England happen to be associated with the two great days on which the stronghold of Canada was saved by land and sea.

The same tide brought in two other men-of-war. Some soldiers of the 29th, who were on board the *Surprise*, were immediately landed, together with the marines from all three vessels. Carleton called for volunteers from the militia to attack the Americans at once; and nearly every man, both of the French- and of the English-speaking corps, stepped forward. There was joy in every heart that the day for striking back had come at last. The columns marched gaily through the gates and deployed into line at the double on the Heights outside. The Americans fired a few hurried shots and then ran for dear life, leaving their dinners cooking, and, in some cases, even their arms behind them. The Plains were covered with flying enemies and strewn with every sort of impediment to flight, from a cannon to a loaf of bread. Quebec had been saved by British sea-power; and, with it, the whole vast dominion of which it was the key.

CHAPTER VI

DELIVERANCE 1776

The Continental Congress had always been anxious to have delegates from the Fourteenth Colony. But as these never came the Congress finally decided to send a special commission to examine the whole civil and military state of Canada and see what could be done. The news of Montgomery's death and defeat was a very unwelcome surprise. But reinforcements were being sent; the Canadians could surely be persuaded; and a Congressional commission must be able to set things right. This commission was a very strong one. Benjamin Franklin was the chairman. Samuel Chase of Maryland and Charles Carroll of Carrollton were the other members. Carroll's brother, the future archbishop of Baltimore, accompanied them as a sort of ecclesiastical diplomatist. Franklin's prestige and the fact that he was to set up a 'free' printing-press in Montreal were to work wonders with the educated classes at once and with the uneducated masses later on. Chase would appeal to all the reasonable 'moderates.' Carroll, a great landlord and the nearest approach yet made to an American millionaire, was expected to charm the Canadian noblesse; while the fact that he and his exceedingly diplomatic brother were devout Roman Catholics was thought to be by itself a powerful argument with the clergy.

When they reached St Johns towards the end of April the commissioners sent on a courier to announce their arrival and prepare for their proper reception in Montreal. But the ferryman at Laprairie positively refused to accept Continental paper money at any price; and it was only when a 'Friend of Liberty' gave him a dollar in silver that he consented to cross the courier over the St Lawrence. The same hitch occurred in Montreal, where the same Friend of Liberty had to pay in silver before the cab-drivers consented to accept a fare either from him or from the commissioners. Even the name of Carroll of Carrollton was conjured with in vain. The French Canadians remembered Bigot's bad French paper. Their worst suspicions were being confirmed about the equally bad American paper. So they demanded nothing but hard cash—*argent dur*. However, the first great obstacle had been successfully overcome; and so, on the strength of five borrowed silver dollars, the accredited commissioners of the Continental Congress of the Thirteen Colonies made their state entry into what they still hoped to call the Fourteenth Colony. But silver dollars were scarce; and on the 1st of May the crestfallen commissioners had to send the Congress a financial report which may best be summed up in a pithy phrase which soon became proverbial—'Not worth a Continental. '

On the 10th of May they heard the bad news from Quebec and increased the panic among their Montreal sympathizers by hastily leaving the city lest they should be cut off by a British man-of-war. Franklin foresaw the end and left for Philadelphia accompanied by the Reverend John Carroll, whose twelve days of disheartening experience with the leading French-Canadian clergy had convinced him that they were impervious to any arguments or blandishments emanating from the Continental Congress. It was a sad disillusionment for the commissioners, who had expected to be settling the affairs of a fourteenth colony instead of being obliged to leave the city from which they were to have enlightened the people with a free press. In their first angry ignorance they laid the whole blame on their unfortunate army for its 'disgraceful flight' from Quebec. A week later, when Chase and Charles Carroll ought to have known better, they were still assuring the Congress that this 'shameful retreat' was 'the principal cause of all the disorders' in the army; and even after the whole story ought to have been understood neither they nor the Congress gave their army its proper due. But, as a matter of fact, the American position had become untenable the moment the British fleet began to threaten the American line of communication with Montreal. For the rest, the American volunteers, all things considered, had done very well indeed. Arnold's march was a truly magnificent feat. Morgan's men had fought with great courage at the Sault-au-Matelot. And though Montgomery's assault might well have been better planned and executed, we must remember that the good plan, which had been rejected, was the military one, while the bad plan, which had been adopted, was concocted by mere politicians. Nor were 'all the disorders' so severely condemned by the commissioners due to the army alone. Far from it, indeed. The root of 'all the disorders' lay in the fact that a makeshift government was obliged to use makeshift levies for an invasion which required a regular army supported by a fleet.

On the 19th of May another disaster happened, this time above Montreal. The Congress had not felt strong enough to attack the western posts. So Captain Forster of the 8th Foot, finding that he was free to go elsewhere, had come down from Oswegatchie (the modern Ogdensburg) with a hundred whites and two hundred Indians and made prisoners of four hundred and thirty Americans at the Cedars, about thirty miles up the St Lawrence from Montreal. Forster was a very good officer. Butterfield, the American commander, was a very bad one. And that made all the difference. After two days of feeble and misdirected defence Butterfield surrendered three hundred and fifty men. The other eighty were reinforcements who walked into the trap next day. Forster now had four American prisoners for every white soldier of his own; while Arnold was near by, having come up from Sorel to Lachine with a small but determined force. So Forster, carefully pointing out to his prisoners their danger if the Indians should be reinforced and run wild, offered them their freedom on condition that they should be regarded as being exchanged for an equal number of British prisoners in American hands. This was agreed to and never made a matter of dispute afterwards. But the second article Butterfield accepted was a stipulation that, while the released British were to be free to fight again, the released Americans were not; and it was over this point that a bitter controversy raged. The British authorities maintained that all the terms were binding because they had been accepted by an officer commissioned by the Congress. The Congress maintained that the disputed article was obtained by an unfair threat of an Indian massacre and that it was so one-sided as to be good for nothing but repudiation.

'The Affair at the Cedars' thus became a sorely vexed question. In itself it would have died out among later and more important issues if it had not been used as a torch to fire American public opinion at a time when the Congress was particularly anxious to make the Thirteen Colonies as anti-British as possible. Most of Forster's men were Indians. He had reminded Butterfield how dangerous an increasing number of Indians might become. Butterfield was naturally anxious to prove that he had yielded only to overwhelming odds and horrifying risks. Americans in general were ready to believe anything bad about the Indians and the British. The temptation and the opportunity seemed made for each other. And so a quite imaginary Indian massacre conveniently appeared in the American news of the day and helped to form the kind of public opinion which was ardently desired by the party of revolt.

The British evidence in this and many another embittering dispute about the Indians need not be cited, since the following items of American evidence do ample justice to both sides. In the spring of

1775 the Massachusetts Provincial Congress sent Samuel Kirkland to exhort the Iroquois 'to whet their hatchet and be prepared to defend our liberties and lives'; while Ethan Allen asked the Indians round Vermont to treat him 'like a brother and ambush the regulars. ' In 1776 the Continental Congress secretly resolved 'that it is highly expedient to engage the Indians in the service of the United Colonies. ' This was before the members knew about the Affair at the Cedars. A few days later Washington was secretly authorized to raise two thousand Indians; while agents were secretly sent 'to engage the Six Nations in our Interest, on the best terms that can be procured. ' Within three weeks of this secret arrangement the Declaration of Independence publicly accused the king of trying 'to bring on the inhabitants of our frontiers the merciless Indian savages. ' Four days after this public accusation the Congress gave orders for raising Indians along 'the Penobscot, the St John, and in Nova Scotia'; and an entry to that effect was made in its Secret Journal. Yet, before the month was out, the same Congress publicly appealed to 'The People of Ireland' in the following words: 'The wild and barbarous savages of the wilderness have been solicited by gifts to take up the hatchet against us, and instigated to deluge our settlements with the blood of defenceless women and children. '

The American defeats at Quebec and at the Cedars completely changed the position of the two remaining commissioners. They had expected to control a victorious advance. They found themselves the highest authority present with a disastrous retreat. Thereupon they made blunder after blunder. Public interest and parliamentary control are the very life of armies and navies in every country which enjoys the blessings of self-government. But civilian interference is death. Yet Chase and Carroll practically abolished rank in the disintegrating army by becoming an open court of appeal to every junior with a grievance or a plan. There never was an occasion on which military rule was more essential in military matters. Yet, though they candidly admitted that they had 'neither abilities nor inclination' to command, these wretched misrulers tried to do their duty both to the Congress and the army by turning the camp into a sort of town meeting where the best orders had no chance whatever against the loudest 'sentiments. ' They had themselves found the root of all evil in the retreat from Quebec. Their army, like every impartial critic, found it in 'the Commissioners and the smallpox' — with the commissioners easily first. The smallpox had been bad enough at Quebec. It became far worse at Sorel. There were few doctors, fewer medicines, and not a single hospital. The reinforcements melted away with the army they were meant to strengthen. Famine threatened both, even in May. Finally the commissioners left for home at the end of the month. But even their departure could no longer make the army's burden light enough to bear.

Thomas, the ex-apothecary, who did his best to stem the adverse tide of trouble, caught the smallpox, became blind, and died at the beginning of June. Sullivan, the fourth commander in less than half a year, having determined that one more effort should be made, arrived at Sorel with new battalions after innumerable difficulties by the way. He was led to believe that Carleton's reinforcements had come from Nova Scotia, not from England; and this encouraged him to push on farther. He was naturally of a very sanguine temper; and Thompson, his second-in-command, heartily approved of the dash. The new troops cheered up and thought of taking Quebec itself. But, after getting misled by their guide, floundering about in bottomless bogs, and losing a great deal of very precious time, they found Three Rivers defended by entrenchments, superior numbers, and the vanguard of the British fleet. Nevertheless they attacked bravely on the 8th of June. But, taken in front and flank by well-drilled regulars and well-handled men-of-war, they presently broke and fled. Every avenue of escape was closed as they wandered about the woods and bogs. But Carleton, who came up from Quebec after the battle was all over, purposely opened the way to Sorel. He had done his best to win the hearts of his prisoners at Quebec and had succeeded so well that when they returned to Crown Point they were kept away from the rest of the American army lest their account of his kindness should affect its anti-British zeal. Now that he was in overwhelming force he thought he saw an even better chance of earning gratitude from rebels and winning converts to the loyal side by a still greater act of clemency.

The battle of Three Rivers was the last action fought on Canadian soil. The American army retreated to Sorel and up the Richelieu to St Johns, where it was joined by Arnold, who had just evacuated Montreal. Most of the Friends of Liberty in Canada fled either with or before their beaten forces. So, like the ebbing of a whole river system, the main and tributary streams of fugitives drew south towards Lake Champlain. The neutral French Canadians turned against them at once; though not to the extent of making an actual attack. The habitant cared nothing for the incomprehensible constitutionalities over which different kinds of British foreigners were fighting their exasperating civil war. But he did know what the king's big fleet and army meant. He did begin to feel that his own ways of life were safer with the loyal than with the rebel side. And he quite understood that he had been forced to give a good deal for nothing ever since the American commissioners had authorized their famishing army to commandeer his supplies and pay him with their worthless 'Continentals. '

From St Johns the worn-out Americans crawled homewards in stray, exhausted parties, dropping fast by the way as they went. 'I did not look into a hut or a tent, ' wrote a horrified observer, 'in which I did not find a dead or dying man. ' Disorganization became so complete that no exact returns were ever made up. But it is known that over ten thousand armed men crossed into Canada from first to last and that not far short of half this total either found their death beyond the line or brought it back with them to Lake Champlain.

It was on what long afterwards became Dominion Day—the 1st of July—that the ruined American forces reassembled at Crown Point, having abandoned all hope of making Canada the Fourteenth Colony. Three days later the disappointed Thirteen issued the Declaration of Independence which virtually proclaimed that Canadians and Americans should thenceforth live a separate life.

CHAPTER VII

THE COUNTERSTROKE 1776-1778

Six thousand British troops, commanded by Burgoyne, and four thousand Germans, commanded by Baron Riedesel, had arrived at Quebec before the battle of Three Rivers. Quebec itself had then been left to the care of a German garrison under a German commandant, 'that excellent man, Colonel Baum, ' while the great bulk of the army had marched up the St Lawrence, as we have seen already. Such a force as this new one of Carleton's was expected to dismay the rebel colonies. And so, to a great extent, it did. With a much larger force in the colonies themselves the king was confidently expected to master his unruly subjects, no matter how much they proclaimed their independence. The Loyalists were encouraged. The trimmers prepared to join them. Only those steadfast Americans who held their cause dearer than life itself were still determined to venture all. But they formed the one party that really knew its own mind. This gave them a great advantage over the king's party, which, hampered at every turn by the opposition in the mother country, was never quite sure whether it ought to strike hard or gently in America.

On one point, however, everybody was agreed. The command of Lake Champlain was essential to whichever side would hold its own. The American forces at Crown Point might be too weak for the time being. But Arnold knew that even ten thousand British soldiers could not overrun the land without a naval force to help them. So he got together a flotilla which had everything its own way during the time that Carleton was laboriously building a rival flotilla on the Richelieu with a very scanty supply of ship-wrights and materials. Arnold, moreover, could devote his whole attention to the work, makeshift as it had to be; while Carleton was obliged to keep moving about the province in an effort to bring it into some sort of order after the late invasion. Throughout the summer the British army held the line of the Richelieu all the way south as far as Isle-aux-Noix, very near the lake and the line. But Carleton's flotilla could not set sail from St Johns till October 5, by which time the main body of his army was concentrated round Pointe-au-Fer, at the northern end of the lake, ninety miles north of the American camp at Crown Point.

It was a curious situation for a civil and military governor to be hoisting his flag as a naval commander-in-chief, however small the fleet might be. But it is commonly ignored that, down to the present day, the governor-general of Canada is appointed 'Vice-Admiral of the Same' in his commissions from the Crown. Carleton of course carried expert naval officers with him and had enough professional seamen to work the vessels and lay the guns. But, though Captain Pringle manoeuvred the flotilla and Lieutenant Dacre handled the flagship *Carleton*, the actual command remained in Carleton's own hands. The capital ship (and the only real square-rigged 'ship') of this Lilliputian fleet was Pringle's *Inflexible*, which had been taken up the Richelieu in sections and hauled past the portages with immense labour before reaching St Johns, whence there is a clear run upstream to Lake Champlain. The *Inflexible* carried thirty guns, mostly 12-pounders, and was an overmatch for quite the half of Arnold's decidedly weaker flotilla. The *Lady Maria* was a sort of sister ship to the *Carleton*. The little armada was completed by a 'gondola' with six 9-pounders, by twenty gunboats and four longboats, each carrying a single piece, and by many small craft used as transports.

On the 11th of October Carleton's whole naval force was sailing south when one of Arnold's vessels was seen making for Valcour Island, a few miles still farther south on the same, or western, side of Lake Champlain. Presently the Yankee ran ashore on the southern end of the island, where she was immediately attacked by some British small craft while the *Inflexible* sailed on. Then, to the intense disgust of the *Inflexible*'s crew, Arnold's complete flotilla was suddenly discovered drawn up in a masterly position between the mainland and the island. It was too late for the *Inflexible* to beat back now. But the rest of Carleton's flotilla turned in to the attack. Arnold's flanks rested on the island and the mainland. His rear could be approached only by beating back against a bad wind all the way round the outside of Valcour Island; and, even if this manoeuvre could have been performed, the British attack on his rear from the north could have been made only in a piecemeal way, because the channel was there at its narrowest, with a bad obstruction in the middle. So, for every reason, a frontal attack from the south was the one way of closing with him. The fight was furious while it lasted and seemingly decisive when it ended. Arnold's best vessel, the *Royal Savage*, which he had taken at St Johns the year before, was driven ashore and captured. The others were so severely mauled that when the victorious British anchored their superior force in line across Arnold's front there seemed to be no chance for him to escape the following day. But that night he performed an even more daring and wonderful feat than Bouchette had performed the year before when paddling Carleton through the American lines among the islands opposite Sorel. Using muffled sweeps, with consummate skill he slipped all his remaining vessels between the mainland and the nearest British gunboat, and was well on his way to Crown Point before his escape had been discovered. Next day Carleton chased south. The day after he destroyed the whole of the enemy's miniature sea-power as a fighting force. But the only three serviceable vessels got away; while Arnold burnt everything else likely to fall into British hands. So Carleton had no more than his own reduced flotilla to depend on when he occupied Crown Point.

A vexed question, destined to form part of a momentous issue, now arose. Should Ticonderoga be attacked at once or not? It commanded the only feasible line of march from Montreal to New York; and no force from Canada could therefore attack the new republic effectively without taking it first. But the season was late. The fort was strong, well gunned, and well manned. Carleton's reconnaissance convinced him that he could have little chance of reducing it quickly, if at all, with the means at hand, especially as the Americans had supplies close by at Lake George, while he was now a hundred miles south of his base. A winter siege was impossible. Sufficient supplies could never be brought through the dense, snow-encumbered bush, all the way from Canada, even if the long and harassing line of communications had not been everywhere open to American attack. Moreover, Carleton's army was in no way prepared for a midwinter campaign, even if it could have been supplied with food and warlike stores. So he very sensibly turned his back on Lake Champlain until the following year.

That was the gayest winter Quebec had seen since Montcalm's first season, twenty years before. Carleton had been knighted for his services and was naturally supposed to be the chosen leader for the next campaign. The ten thousand troops gave confidence to the loyalists and promised success for the coming campaign. The clergy were getting their disillusioned parishioners back to the fold beneath the Union Jack; while *Jean Ba'tis'e* himself was fain to admit that his own ways of life and the money he got for his goods were very much safer with *les Angla's* than with the revolutionists, whom he called *les Bastonna's* because most trade between Quebec and the Thirteen Colonies was carried on by vessels hailing from the port of Boston. The seigneurs were delighted. They still hoped for commissions as regulars, which too few of them ever received; and they were charmed with the little viceregal court over which Lady Maria

Carleton, despite her youthful two-and-twenty summers, presided with a dignity inherited from the premier ducal family of England and brought to the acme of conventional perfection by her intimate experience of Versailles. On New Year's Eve Carleton gave a public fete, a state dinner, and a ball to celebrate the anniversary of the British victory over Montgomery and Arnold. The bishop held a special thanksgiving and made all notorious renegades do open penance. Nothing seemed wanting to bring the New Year in under the happiest auspices since British rule began.

But, quite unknown to Carleton, mischief was brewing in the Colonial Office of that unhappy government which did so many stupid things and got the credit for so many more. In 1775 the well-meaning Earl of Dartmouth was superseded by Lord George Germain, who continued the mismanagement of colonial affairs for seven disastrous years. Few characters have abused civil and military positions more than the man who first, as a British general, disgraced the noble name of Sackville on the battlefield of Minden in 1759, and then, as a cabinet minister, disgraced throughout America the plebeian one of Germain, which he took in 1770 with a suitable legacy attached to it. His crime at Minden was set down by the thoughtless public to sheer cowardice. But Sackville was no coward. He had borne himself with conspicuous gallantry at Fontenoy. He was admired, before Minden, by two very brave soldiers, Wolfe and the Duke of Cumberland. And he afterwards fought a famous duel with as much sang-froid as any one would care to see. His real crime at Minden was admirably exposed by the court-martial which found him 'guilty of having disobeyed the orders of Prince Ferdinand of Brunswick, whom he was by his commission bound to obey as commander-in-chief, according to the rules of war. ' This court also found him 'unfit to serve his Majesty in any military capacity whatever'; and George II directed that the following 'remarks' should be added when the sentence was read out on parade to every regiment in the service: 'It is his Majesty's pleasure that the above sentence be given out in public orders, not only in Britain, but in America, and in every quarter of the globe where British troops happen to be, so that all officers, being convinced that neither high birth nor great employments can shelter offences of such a nature, and seeing they are subject to censures worse than death to a man who has any sense of honour, may avoid the fatal consequences arising from disobedience of orders. '

This seemed to mark the end of Sackville's sinister career. But when George II died and George III began to reign, with a very different set of men to help him, the bad general reappeared as an equally bad politician. Haughty, cantankerous, and self-opinionated to the last degree, Germain, who had many perverse abilities fitting him for the meaner side of party politics, was appointed to the post for which he was least qualified just when Canada and the Thirteen Colonies most needed a master mind. Worse still, he cherished a contemptible grudge against Carleton for having refused to turn out a good officer and put in a bad one who happened to be a pampered favourite. At first, however, Carleton was allowed to do his best. But in the summer of 1776 Germain restricted Carleton's command to Canada and put Burgoyne, a junior officer, in command of the army destined to make the counterstroke. The ship bearing this malicious order had to put back; so it was not till the middle of May 1777 that Carleton was disillusioned by its arrival as well as by a second and still more exasperating dispatch accusing him of neglect of duty for not having taken Ticonderoga in November and thus prevented Washington from capturing the Hessians at Trenton. The physical impossibility of a winter siege, the three hundred miles of hostile country between Trenton and Ticonderoga, and the fact that the other leading British general, Howe, had thirty thousand troops in the Colonies, while Carleton had only ten thousand with which to hold Canada that year and act as ordered next year, all went for nothing when Germain found a chance to give a good stab in the back.

On May 20 Carleton wrote a pungent reply, pointing out the utter impossibility of following up his victory on Lake Champlain by carrying out Germain's arm-chair plan of operations in the middle of winter. 'I regard it as a particular blessing that your Lordship's dispatch did not arrive in due time. ' As for the disaster at Trenton, he 'begs to inform his Lordship' that if Howe's thirty thousand men had been properly used the Hessians could never have been taken, 'though all the rebels from Ticonderoga had reinforced Mr Washington's army. ' Moreover, 'I never could imagine why, if troops so far south [as Howe's] found it necessary to go into winter quarters, your Lordship could possibly expect troops so far north to continue their operations. ' A week later Carleton wrote again and sent in his resignation. 'Finding that I can no longer be of use, under your Lordship's administration... I flatter myself I shall obtain the king's permission to return home this fall.... I shall embark with great satisfaction, still entertaining the ardent wish that, after my departure, the dignity of the Crown in this unfortunate Province may not appear beneath your Lordship's concern. '

Burgoyne had spent the winter in London and had arrived at Quebec about the same time as Germain's dispatches. He had loyally represented Carleton's plans at headquarters. But he did not know America and he was not great enough to see the weak points in the plan which Germain proposed to carry out with wholly inadequate means.

There was nothing wrong with the actual idea of this plan. Washington, Carleton, and every other leading man on either side saw perfectly well that the British army ought to cut the rebels in two by holding the direct line from Montreal to New York throughout the coming campaign of 1777. Given the irresistible British command of the sea, fifty thousand troops were enough. The general idea was that half of these should hold the four-hundred-mile line of the Richelieu, Lake Champlain, and the Hudson, while the other half seized strategic points elsewhere and still further divided the American forces. But the troops employed were ten thousand short of the proper number. Many of them were foreign mercenaries. And the generals were not the men to smash the enemy at all costs. They were ready to do their duty. But their affinities were rather with the opposition, which was against the war, than with the government, which was for it. Howe was a strong Whig. Burgoyne became a follower of Fox. Clinton had many Whig connections. Cornwallis voted against colonial taxation. To make matters worse, the government itself wavered between out-and-out war and some sort of compromise both with its political opponents at home and its armed opponents in America.

Under these circumstances Carleton was in favour of a modified plan. Ticonderoga had been abandoned by the Americans and occupied by the British as Burgoyne marched south. Carleton's idea was to use it as a base of operations against New England, while Howe's main body struck at the main body of the rebels and broke them up as much as possible. Germain however, was all for the original plan. So Burgoyne set off for the Hudson, expecting to get into touch with Howe at Albany. But Germain, in his haste to leave town for a holiday, forgot to sign Howe's orders at the proper time; and afterwards forgot them altogether. So Howe, pro-American in politics and temporizer in the field, manoeuvred round his own headquarters at New York until October, when he sailed south to

Philadelphia. Receiving no orders from Germain, and having no initiative of his own, he had made no attempt to hold the line of the Hudson all the way north to Albany, where he could have met Burgoyne and completed the union of the forces which would have cut the Colonies in two. Meanwhile Burgoyne, ignorant of Germain's neglect and Howe's futilities, was struggling to his fate at Saratoga, north of Albany. He had been receiving constant aid from Carleton's scanty resources, though Carleton knew full well that the sending of any aid beyond the limits of the province exposed him to personal ruin in case of a reverse in Canada. But it was all in vain; and, on the 17th of October, Burgoyne—much more sinned against than sinning—laid down his arms. The British garrison immediately evacuated Ticonderoga and retired to St Johns, thus making Carleton's position fairly safe in Canada. But Germain, only too glad to oust him, had now notified him that Haldimand, the new governor, was on the point of sailing for Quebec. Haldimand, to his great credit, had asked to have his own appointment cancelled when he heard of Germain's shameful attitude towards Carleton, and had only consented to go after being satisfied that Carleton really wished to come home. The exchange, however, was not to take place that year. Contrary winds blew Haldimand back; and so Canada had to remain under the best of all possible governors in spite of Germain.

Germain had provoked Carleton past endurance both by his public blunders and by his private malice. Even in 1776 there was hate on one side, contempt on the other. When Germain had blamed Carleton for not carrying out the idiotic winter siege of Ticonderoga, Carleton, in his official reply, 'could only suppose' that His Lordship had acted 'in other places with such great wisdom that, without our assistance, the rebels must immediately be compelled to lay down their arms and implore the King's mercy. ' After that Germain had murder in his heart to the bitter end of Carleton's rule. Carleton had frequently reported the critical state of affairs in Canada. 'There is nothing to fear from the Canadians so long as things are in a state of prosperity; nothing to hope from them when in distress. There are some of them who are guided by sentiments of honour. The multitude is influenced by hope of gain or fear of punishment. ' The recent invasion had proved this up to the hilt. Then welcome reaction began. The defeat of the invaders, the arrival of Burgoyne's army, and the efforts of the seigneurs and the clergy had considerably brightened the prospects of the British cause in Canada. The partial mobilization of the militia which followed Burgoyne's surrender was not, indeed, a great success. But it was far better than the fiasco of two years before. There was also a corresponding improvement in civil life. The judges whom Carleton had been obliged to appoint in haste all proved at leisure the wisdom of his choice; and there seemed to be every chance that other nominees would be equally fit for their positions, because the Quebec Act, which annulled every appointment made before it came into force, opened the way for the exclusion of bad officials and the inclusion of the good.

But the chance of perverting this excellent intention was too much for Germain, who succeeded in foisting one worthless nominee after another on the province just as Carleton was doing his best to heal old sores. One of the worst cases was that of Livius, a low-down, money-grubbing German Portuguese, who ousted the future Master of the Rolls; Sir William Grant, a man most admirably fitted to interpret the laws of Canada with knowledge, sympathy, and absolute impartiality. Livius as chief justice was more than Carleton could stand in silence. This mongrel lawyer had picked up all the Yankee vices without acquiring any of the countervailing Yankee virtues. He was 'greedy of power, more greedy of gain, imperious and impetuous in his temper, but learned in the ways and eloquence of the New England provinces, and valuing himself particularly on his knowledge of how to manage governors. ' He had been sent by Germain 'to administer justice to the Canadians when he understands neither their laws, manners, customs, nor language. ' Other like nominees followed, 'characters regardless of the public tranquility but zealous to pay court to a powerful minister and— provided they can obtain advantages—unconcerned should the means of obtaining them prove ruinous to the King's service. ' These pettifoggers so turned and twisted the law about for the sake of screwing out the maximum of fees that Carleton pointedly refused to appoint Livius as a member of the Legislative Council. Livius then laid his case before the Privy Council in England. But this great court of ultimate appeal pronounced such a damning judgment on his gross pretensions that even Germain could not prevent his final dismissal from all employment under the Crown.

Wounded in the house of those who should have been his friends, thwarted in every measure of his self-sacrificing rule, Carleton served on devotedly through six weary months of 1778—the year in which a vindictive government of Bourbon France became the first of the several foreign enemies who made the new American republic an accomplished fact by taking sides in a British civil war. His burden was now far more than any man could bear. Yet he closed his answer to Germain's parting shot with words which are as noble as his deeds:

'I have long looked out for the arrival of a successor. Happy at last to learn his near approach, I resign the important commands with which I have been entrusted into hands less obnoxious to your Lordship. Thus, for the King's service, as willingly I lay them down as, for his service, I took them up. '

CHAPTER VIII

GUARDING THE LOYALISTS 1782-1783

Burgoyne's surrender marked the turning of the tide against the British arms. True, the three campaigns of purely civil war, begun in 1775, had reached no decisive result. True also that the Independence declared in 1776 had no apparent chance of becoming an accomplished fact. But 1777 was the fatal year for all that. The long political strife in England, the gross mismanagement of colonial affairs under Germain, and the shameful blunders that made Saratoga possible, all combined to encourage foreign powers to take the field against the king's incompetent and distracted ministry. France, Spain, and Holland joined the Americans in arms; while Russia, Sweden, Denmark, Prussia, and all the German seaboard countries formed the Armed Neutrality of the North. This made stupendous odds—no less than ten to one. First of the ten came the political opposition at home, which, in regard to the American rebellion itself, was at least equal to the most powerful enemy abroad. Next came the four enemies in arms: the American rebels, France, Spain, and Holland. Finally came the five armed neutrals, all ready to use their navies on the slightest provocation.

From this it may be seen that not one-half, perhaps not a quarter, of all the various forces that won the Revolutionary war were purely American. Nor were the Americans and their allies together victorious over the mother country, but only over one sorely hampered party in it. Yet, from the nature of the case, the Americans got much more than the lion's share of the spoils, while, even in their own eyes, they seemed to have gained honour and glory in the same proportion. The last real campaign was fought in 1781 and ended with the British surrender at Yorktown. From that time on peace was in the air. The unfortunate ministry, now on the eve of political defeat at home, were sick of civil war and only too anxious for a chance of uniting all parties against the foreign foes. But they had first to settle with the Americans, who had considered themselves an independent sovereign power for the last five years and who were determined to make the most of England's difficulties. No darker New Year's Day had ever dawned on any cabinet than that of 1782 on North's. In spite of his change from repression to conciliation, and in spite of dismissing Germain to the House of Lords with an ill-earned peerage, Lord North found his majority dwindling away. At last, on the 20th of March, he resigned.

Meanwhile every real statesman in either party had felt that the crisis required the master-hand of Carleton. With Germain, the empire-wrecker, gone, Carleton would doubtless have served under any cabinet, for no government could have done without him. But his actual commission came through the Rockingham administration on the 4th of April. After three quiet years of retirement at his country seat in Hampshire he was again called upon to face a situation of extreme difficulty. For once, with a wisdom rare enough in any age and almost unknown in that one, the government gave him a free hand and almost unlimited powers. The only questions over which he had no final power were those of making treaties. He was appointed 'General and Commander-in-chief of all His Majesty's forces within the Colonies lying in the Atlantic Ocean, from Nova Scotia to the Floridas, and inclusive of Newfoundland and Canada should they be attacked. ' He was also appointed commissioner for executing the terms of any treaty that might be made; and his instructions contained two passages which bore eloquent witness to the universal confidence reposed in him. 'It is impossible to judge of the precise situation at so great a distance' and 'His Majesty's affairs are so situated that further deliberations give way to instant decision. We are satisfied that whatever inconveniences may arise they will be compensated by the presence of a commander-in-chief of whose discretion, conduct, and ability His Majesty has long entertained the highest opinion. ' Thus the great justifier of British rule beyond the seas arrived in New York on the 9th of May 1782 with at least some hope of reconciling enough Americans to turn the scale before it was too late.

For three months the prospect, though worse than he had anticipated, did not seem utterly hopeless. It had been considerably brightened by Rodney's great victory over the French fleet which was on its way to attack Jamaica. But an unfortunate incident happened to be exasperating Loyalists and revolutionists at this very time. Some revolutionists had killed a Loyalist named Philip White, apparently out of pure hate. Some Loyalists, under Captain Lippincott, then seized and hanged Joshua Huddy, a captain in the Congress militia, out of sheer revenge. A paper left pinned on Huddy's breast bore the inscription: 'Up goes Huddy for Philip White. ' Washington then demanded that Lippincott should be delivered up; and, on Carleton's refusal, chose a British prisoner by lot instead. The lot fell on a young Lieutenant Asgill of the Guards, whose mother appealed to the king and queen of France and to their powerful minister, Vergennes. The American Congress wanted blood for blood, which would have led to an endless vendetta. But Vergennes pointed out that Asgill, a youth of nineteen, was as much a prisoner of the king of France as of the Continental Congress. At this the Congress gnashed its teeth, but had to give way.

While the Asgill affair was still running its course, and embittering Loyalists and rebels more than ever, Carleton was suddenly informed that the government had decided to grant complete independence. This was more than he could stand; and he at once asked to be recalled. He had been all for honourable reconciliation from the first. He had been particularly kind to his American prisoners in Canada and had purposely refrained from annihilating the American army after the battle of Three Rivers. But he was not prepared for independence. Nor had he been sent out with this ostensible object in view. His official instructions were to inform the Americans that 'the most liberal sentiments had taken root in the nation, and that the narrow policy of monopoly was totally extinguished. ' Now he was called upon to surrender without having tried either his arms or his diplomacy. With British sea-power beginning to reassert its age-long superiority over all possible rivals, with practically all constitutional points of dispute conceded to the revolutionists, and with the certain knowledge that by no means the majority of all Americans were absolute anti-British out-and-outers, he thought it no time to dismember the Empire. His Intelligence Department had been busily collecting information which seems surprising enough as we read it over to-day, but which was based on the solid facts of that unhappy time. One member of the Continental Congress was anxious to know what would become of the American army if reconciliation should be effected on the understanding that there would be no more imperial taxation or customs duty—would it become part of the Imperial Army, or what?

But speculation on all such contingencies was suddenly cut short by the complete change of policy at home. The idea was to end the civil war that had divided the Empire and to concentrate on the foreign war that at least united the people of Great Britain. No matter at what cost this policy had now to be carried out; and Carleton was the only man that every one would trust to do it. So, sacrificing his own feelings and convictions, he made the best of an exceedingly bad business. He had to safeguard the prisoners and Loyalists while preparing to evacuate the few remaining footholds of British power in the face of an implacable foe. At the same time he had to watch every other point in North America and keep in touch with his excellent naval colleague, Admiral Digby, lest his own rear might be attacked by the three foreign enemies of England. He was even ordered off to the West Indies in the autumn. But counter-orders fortunately arrived before he could start. Thus, surrounded by enemies in front and rear and on both flanks, he spent the seven months between August and the following March.

At the end of March 1783 news arrived that the preliminary treaty of peace had been signed. The final treaty was not signed till his fifty-ninth birthday, the 3rd of the following September. The signature of the preliminaries simplified the naval and military situation. But it made the situation of the Loyalists worse than ever. Compared with them the prisoners of war had been most highly favoured from the first. And yet the British prisoners had little to thank the Congress for. That they were badly fed and badly housed was not always the fault of the Americans. But that political favourites and underlings were allowed to prey on them was an inexcusable disgrace. When a prisoner complained, he was told it was the fault of the British government which would not pay for his keep! This answer, so contrary to all the accepted usages of war, which reserve such payments till after the conclusion of peace, was no empty gibe; for when, some time before the preliminaries had been signed, the British and American commissioners met to effect an exchange of prisoners, the Americans began by claiming the immediate payment of what the British prisoners had cost them. This of course broke up the meeting at once. In the meantime the German prisoners in British pay were offered their freedom at eighty dollars a head. Then farmers came forward to buy up these prisoners at this price. But the farmers found competitors in the recruiting sergeants, who urged the Germans, with only too much truth, not to become 'the slaves of farmers' but to follow 'the glorious trade of war' against their employers, the British government. To their honour be it said, these Germans kept faith with the British, much to the surprise of the Americans, who, like many modern writers, could not understand that these foreign mercenaries took a professional pride in carrying out a sworn contract, even when it would pay them better to break it. The British prisoners were not put up for sale in the same way. But money sent to them had a habit of disappearing on the road—one item mentioned by Carleton amounted to six thousand pounds.

If such was the happy lot of prisoners during the war, what was the wretched lot of Loyalists after the treaty of peace? The words of one of the many petitions sent in to Carleton will suggest the answer. 'If we have to encounter this inexpressible misfortune we beg consideration for our lives, fortunes, and property, *and not by mere terms of treaty.* ' What this means cannot be appreciated unless we fully realize how strong the spirit of hate and greed had grown, and why it had grown so strong.

The American Revolution had not been provoked by oppression, violence, and massacre. The 'chains and slavery' of revolutionary orators was only a figure of speech. The real causes were constitutional and personal; and the actual crux of the question was one of payment for defence. Of course there were many other causes at work. The social, religious, and political grudges with which so many emigrants had left the mother country had not been forgotten and were now revived. Commercial restrictions, however well they agreed with the spirit of the age, were galling to such keen traders. And the mere difference between colonies and motherland had produced misunderstandings on both sides. But the main provocative cause was Imperial taxation for local defence. The Thirteen Colonies could not have held their own by land or sea, much less could they have conquered their French rivals, without the Imperial forces, which, indeed, had done by far the greater part of the fighting. How was the cost to be shared between the mother country and themselves? The colonies had not been asked to pay more than their share. The point was whether they could be taxed at all by the Imperial government when they had no representation in the Imperial parliament. The government said Yes. The colonies and the opposition at home said No. As the colonies would not pay of their own accord, and as the government did not see why they should be parasites on the armed strength of the mother country, parliament proceeded to tax them. They then refused to pay under compulsion; and a complete deadlock ensued.

The personal factors in this perhaps insoluble problem were still more refractory than the constitutional. All the great questions of peace and war and other foreign relations were settled by the mother country, which was the only sovereign power and which alone possessed the force to make any British rights respected. The Americans supplied subordinate means and so became subordinate men when they and the Imperial forces worked together. This, to use a homely phrase, made their leaders feel out of it. Everything that

The Father of British Canada: A Chronicle of Carleton

breeds trouble between militiamen and regulars, colonials and mother-countrymen, fanned the flame of colonial resentment till the leaders were able to set their followers on fire. It was a leaders' rebellion: there was no maddening cruelty or even oppression such as those which have produced so many revolutions elsewhere. It was a leaders' victory: there was no general feeling that death or independence were the only alternatives from the first. But as the fight went on, and Loyalists and revolutionists grew more and more bitter towards one another, the revolutionary followers found the same cause for hating the Loyalists as their leaders had found for hating the government. Many of the Loyalists belonged to the well-educated and well-to-do classes. So the envy and greed of the revolutionary followers were added to the personal and political rage of their leaders.

The British government had done its best for the Loyalists in the treaty of peace and had urged Carleton, who needed no urging in such a cause, to do his best as well. But the treaty was made with the Congress; and the Congress had no authority over the internal affairs of the thirteen new states, each one of which could do as it liked with its own envied and detested Loyalists. The revolutionists wanted some tangible spoils. The safety of peace had made the trimmers equally 'patriotic' and equally clamorous. So the confiscation of Loyalist property soon became the order of the day.

It was not the custom of that age to confiscate private property simply because the owners were on the losing side, still less to confiscate it under local instead of national authority. But need, greed, and resentment were stronger than any scruples. Need was the weakest, resentment the strongest of all the animating motives. The American army was in rags and its pay greatly in arrears while the British forces under Carleton were fed, clothed, and paid in the regular way. But it was the passionate resentment of the revolutionists that perverted this exasperating difference into another 'intolerable wrong. ' Washington was above such meaner measures. But when he said the Loyalists were only fit for suicide, and when Adams, another future president, said they ought to be hanged, it is little wonder that lesser men thought the time had come for legal looting. Those Loyalists who best understood the temper of their late fellow-countrymen left at once. They were right. Even to be a woman was no protection against confiscation in the case of Mary Phillips, sister-in-law to Beverley Robinson, a well-known Loyalist who settled in New Brunswick after the Revolution. Her case was

80

not nearly so hard as many another. But her historic love-affair makes it the most romantic. Eight-and-twenty years before this General Braddock had marched to death and defeat beside the Monongahela with two handsome and gallant young aides-de-camp, Washington and Morris. Both fell in love with bewitching Mary Phillips. But, while Washington left her fancy-free, Morris won her heart and hand. Now that the strife was no longer against a foreign foe but between two British parties, the former aides-de-camp found themselves rivals in arms as well as love; for Colonel Morris was Carleton's right-hand man in all that concerned the Loyalists, being the official head of the department of Claims and Succour:

Morris, Morgan, and Carleton were the three busiest men in New York. Forty thick manuscript volumes still show Maurice Morgan's assiduous work as Carleton's confidential secretary. But Morris had the more heart-breaking duty of the three, with no relief, day after sorrow-laden day, from the anguishing appeals of Loyalist widows, orphans, and other ruined refugees. No sooner had the dire news arrived that peace had been made with the Congress, and that each of the thirteen United States was free to show uncovenanted mercies towards its own Loyalists, than the exodus began. Five thousand five hundred and ninety-three Loyalists sailed for Halifax in the first convoy on the 17th of April with a strong recommendation from Carleton to Governor Parr of Nova Scotia. 'Many of these are of the first families and born to the fairest possessions. I therefore beg that you will have them properly considered. ' Shipping was scarce; for the hostility of the whole foreign naval world had made enormous demands on the British navy and mercantile marine. So six thousand Loyalists had to march overland to join Carleton's vessels at New York, some of them from as far south as Charlottesville, Virginia. They were carefully shepherded by Colonel Alured Clarke, of whom we shall hear again.

Meanwhile Carleton and Washington had exchanged the usual compliments on the conclusion of peace and had met each other on the 6th of May at Tappan, where they discussed the exchange of prisoners. By the terms of the treaty the British were to evacuate New York, their last foothold in the new republic, with all practicable dispatch; so, as summer changed into autumn, the Congress became more and more impatient to see the last of them. But Carleton would not go without the Loyalists, whose many tributary streams of misery were still flowing into New York. In September, when the treaty of peace was ratified in Europe, the

Congress asked Carleton point-blank to name the date of his own departure. But he replied that this was impossible and that the more the Loyalists were persecuted the longer he would be obliged to stay. The correspondence between him and the Congress teems with complaints and explanations. The Americans were very anxious lest the Loyalists should take away any goods and chattels not their own, particularly slaves. Carleton was disposed to consider slaves as human beings, though slavery was still the law in the British oversea dominions, and so the Americans felt uneasy lest he might discriminate between their slaves and other chattels. Reams of the Carleton papers are covered with descriptive lists of claimed and counter-claimed niggers—Julius Caesars, Jupiters, Venuses, Dianas, and so on, who were either 'stout wenches' and 'likely fellows' or 'incurably lazy' and 'old worn-outs. '

Perhaps, when a slave wished to remain British, and his case was nicely balanced between the claimants and the counter-claimants, Carleton was a little inclined to give him the benefit of the doubt. But with other forms of disputed property he was too severe to please all Loyalists. A typical case of restitution in Canada will show how differently the two governments viewed the rights of private property. Mercier and Halsted, two Quebec rebels, owned a wharf and the frame of a warehouse in 1775. It was Arnold's intercepted letter to Mercier that gave Carleton's lieutenant, Cramahe, the first warning of danger from the south. Halsted was Major Caldwell's miller at the time and took advantage of his position to give his employer's flour to Arnold's army, in which he served as commissary throughout the siege. Just after the peace of 1783 Mercier and Halsted laid claim to their former property, which they had abandoned for eight years and on which the government had meanwhile built a provision store, making use of the original frame. The case was complicated by many details too long for notice here. But the British government finally gave the two rebels the original property, plus thirteen years' rent, less the cost of government works erected in the meantime. All the documents are still in Quebec.

Property was troublesome enough. But people were worse. And Carleton's difficulties increased as the autumn wore on. The first great harrying of the Loyalists drove more than thirty thousand from their homes; and about twenty-five thousand of these embarked at New York. Then there were the remnants of twenty Loyalist corps to pension, settle, or employ. There were also the British prisoners to receive, besides ten thousand German mercenaries. Add to all this the regular garrison and the general oversight of every British interest in North America, from the Floridas to Labrador, remember the implacable enemy in front, and we may faintly imagine what Carleton had to do before he could report that 'His Majesty's troops and such remaining Loyalists as chose to emigrate were successfully withdrawn on the 25th [of November] without the smallest circumstance of irregularity. '

Thus ended one of the greatest acts in the drama of the British Empire, the English-speaking peoples, or the world; and thus, for the second time, Carleton, now in his sixtieth year, apparently ended his own long service in America. He had left Canada, after saving her from obliteration, because, so long as he remained her governor, the war minister at home remained her enemy. He had then returned to serve in New York, and had stayed there to the bitter end, because there was no other man whom the new government would trust to command the rearguard of the Empire in retreat.

CHAPTER IX

FOUNDING MODERN CANADA 1786-1796

Carleton now enjoyed two years of uninterrupted peace at his country seat in England. His active career seemed to have closed at last. He had no taste for party politics. He was not anxious to fill any position of civil or military trust, even if it had been pressed upon him. And he had said farewell to America for good and all when he had left New York. Though as full of public spirit as before and only just turned sixty, he bid fair to spend the rest of his life as an English country gentleman. His young wife was well contented with her lot. His manly boys promised to become worthy followers of the noble profession of arms. And the overseeing of his little estate occupied his time very pleasantly indeed. Like most healthy Englishmen he was devoted to horses, and, unlike some others, he was very successful with his thoroughbreds.

He had first bought a place near Maidenhead, beside the Thames, which is nowhere lovelier than in that sylvan neighbourhood. Then he bought the present family seat of Greywill Hill near the little village of Odiham in Hampshire. As an ex-governor and commander-in-chief, a county magnate, a personage of great importance to the Empire, and the one victorious British general in the unhappy American war, he had more than earned a peerage. But it was not till 1786, on the eve of his sixty-second birthday, and at a time when his services were urgently required again, that he received it. Needless to say this peerage had nothing whatever to do with his acceptance of another self-sacrificing duty. It was not given till several months after he had promised to return to Canada; and he would certainly have refused it if it had been held out to him as an inducement to go there. He became Baron Dorchester and was granted the not very extravagant addition to his income of a thousand pounds a year payable during four lives, his own, his wife's, and those of his two eldest sons. His elevation to the House of Lords met with the almost unanimous approval of his fellow-peers, in marked contrast to the open hostility they had shown towards his old enemy, Lord George Germain, when that vile wrecker had been 'kicked upstairs' among them. The Carleton motto, crest, and supporters are all most appropriate. The crest is a strong right arm with the hand clenched firmly on an arrow. The motto is *Quondam his vicimus armis—We used to conquer with these arms*. The supporters are two beavers, typifying Canada, while their respective collars, one a naval the other a military coronet, show how her British life was won and saved and has been kept.

Carleton was a man of great reserve and self-control. But his kindly nature must have responded to the cordial welcome which he received on his return to Quebec in October 1786. It was not without reason that the people of Canada rejoiced to have him back as their leader. All that the Indians imagined the Great White Father to be towards themselves he was in reality towards both red man and white. Stern, when the occasion forced him to be stern, just in all his dealings between man and man, dignified and courteous in all his ways, a soldier through every inch of his stalwart six feet, he was a ruler with whom no one ever dreamt of taking liberties. But neither did any deserving one in trouble ever hesitate to lay the most confidential case before him in the full assurance that his head and heart were at the service of all committed to his care. And no other governor, before his time or since, ever inspired his followers with such a firm belief that all would turn out for the best so long as he was in command.

This power of inspiring confidence was now badly needed. Everything in Canada was still provisional. Owing to the war the Quebec Act of 1774 had never been thoroughly enforced. Then, when the war was over, the Loyalists arrived and completely changed the circumstances which the act had been designed to meet. The next constitution, the Canada Act of 1791, was of a very different character. During the seventeen years between these two constitutions all that could be done was to make the best of a very confusing state of flux. Not that the Quebec Act was a dead letter— far from it—but simply that it could not go beyond restoring the privileges of the French-Canadian priests and seigneurs within the area then effectively occupied by the French-Canadian race. Carleton, as we have seen, had faced its problem for the first four years. Haldimand had carried on the government under its provisions for the following six. Hamilton and Hope, successive lieutenant-governors, had bridged the two years between Haldimand's retirement and Carleton's second appointment. Now Carleton was to pick up the threads and make what he could of the tangled skein for the next five years. Haldimand had not been popular with either of the two chief parties into which the leading French Canadians were divided. The seigneurs had nothing like the same regard for a Swiss soldier of fortune that they had for aristocratic British commanders like Murray and Carleton. The clergy also preferred these Anglicans to such a strong Swiss Protestant. The habitants and agitators, who were far less favourable to the new regime, had passionately resented Haldimand's firmness at times of crisis. But, despite all this French-Canadian animus, he was not such an absolute martinet as some writers would have us think. The war with France and with the American Revolutionists required strong government in Canada; while the influx of Loyalists had introduced an entirely new set of most perplexing circumstances. On the whole, Haldimand had done very well in spite of many personal and public drawbacks; and it was through no special fault of his, nor yet of Hope's, that the threads which Carleton picked up formed such a perversely tangled skein.

The troubles that now dogged the great conciliator's every step were of all kinds—racial, religious, social, political, military, diplomatic, legal. The confusion resulting from the intermixture of French and English civil laws had become a great deal more confounded since he had left Canada eight years before. The old proportions of races and religions to each other had changed most disturbingly. The Loyalists were of quite a different social class from the English-speaking immigrants of earlier days. They wanted a parliament, public schools, and many other things new to the country; and they were the sort of people who had a right to have them. The problem of defence was always a vexed one with the inadequate military forces at hand and the insuperable difficulties concerning the militia. The British still held the Western forts pending the settlement of the frontier and the execution of the treaty of peace in full. This naturally annoyed the American government and gave Carleton endless trouble. But more serious still was the ceaseless western march of the American backwoodsmen, who were everywhere in conflict with the Indians. The Indians, in their turn, were confused between the British and Americans under the new conditions. They and their ever-receding rights and territories had not been mentioned in the treaty. But, seeing that they would be better off under British than under American rule, they were inclined to take sides accordingly. There were now no openly hostile sides to take. But, for all that, the British posts in the hinterland looked like weak little islands which might be suddenly engulfed in the sea of Indian troubles raging round them. Then, at the other end of the British line, there were the three maritime provinces to watch over. New Brunswick had been divided off from Nova Scotia and Prince Edward Island had been taken from the direct supervision of the home authorities and placed under the command of the new governor at Quebec. Thus Carleton had to deal directly with everything that happened from the far West to Gaspe, while dealing indirectly with the three maritime provinces and all the troubles that proved too much for their own lieutenant-governors. There was no chance of concentrating on one thing at a time. Nothing would wait. The governor had to watch the writhing tangle as a whole during every minute he devoted to any one kinked and knotted thread.

Fortunately there were some good men in office on both sides of the Atlantic. Lords Sydney and Grenville, the two cabinet ministers with whom Carleton had most to do, were both sensible and sympathetic. Years afterwards Grenville, the favourite cousin of Pitt, became the colleague of Fox at the head of the celebrated 'Ministry of All the Talents. ' Hope was an acceptable lieutenant-governor, and his successor, Sir Alured Clarke, was better still. Francois Bailly, the coadjutor Roman Catholic bishop of Quebec, who had gone to England as French tutor to Carleton's children, was a most enlightened cleric. So too was Charles Inglis, the Anglican bishop of Nova Scotia, appointed in 1787. He was the first Canadian bishop of the Anglican communion and his diocese comprised the whole of British North America. William Smith, the new chief justice, was as different from Carleton's last chief justice, Livius, as angels are from devils. Smith had been an excellent chief justice of his native New York in the old colonial days, and, like Inglis, was a very ardent Loyalist. He respected all reasonable French-Canadian peculiarities. But he favoured the British-Constitutional way of 'broadening down from precedent to precedent' rather than the French way of referring to a supposedly infallible written regulation. We shall soon meet him as a far-seeing statesman. But he well deserves an honoured place in Canadian history for his legal services alone. To him, more than to any other man, is due the nicely balanced adjustments which eventually harmonized the French and English codes into a body of laws adapted to the extraordinary circumstances of the province of Quebec.

Besides the committee on laws Carleton had nominated three other active committees of his council, one on police, another on education, and a third on trade and commerce. The police committee was of the usual kind and dealt with usual problems in the usual way. But the education committee brought out all the vexed questions of French and English, Protestant and Roman Catholic, progressive and reactionary. Strangely enough, the sharpest personal controversy was that between Hubert, the Roman Catholic bishop of Quebec, and his coadjutor Bailly. Hubert enumerated all the institutions already engaged in educational work and suggested that 'rest and be thankful' was the only proper attitude for the committee to assume. But Bailly very neatly pointed out that his respected superior's real opinions could not be those attributed to him over his own signature because they were at variance with the facts. Hubert had said that the cures were spreading education with most commendable zeal, had repudiated the base insinuation that only three or four people in each parish could read and write, and had wound up by thinking that while there was so much land to clear the farmers would do better to keep their sons at home than send them to a university, where they would be under professors so 'unprejudiced' as to have no definite views on religion. Bailly argued that the bishop could not mean what these words seemed to imply, as the logical conclusion would be to wait till Canada was cleared right up to the polar circle. In the end the committee made three very sanguine recommendations: a free common school in every parish, a secondary school in every town or district, and an absolutely non-sectarian central university. This educational ladder was never set up. There was nothing to support either end of it. The financial side was one difficulty. The Jesuits' estates were intended to be made over into educational endowments under government control. But Amherst's claim that they had been granted to him in 1760 was not settled for forty years; and by that time all chance of carrying out the committee's intentions was seen to be hopeless.

Commerce was another burning question and one of much more immediate concern. In 1791 the united populations of all the provinces amounted to only a quarter of a million, of whom at least one-half were French Canadians. Quebec and Montreal had barely ten thousand citizens apiece. But the commercial classes, mostly English-speaking, had greatly increased in numbers, ability, and social standing. The camp-following gangs of twenty years before had now either disappeared or sunk down to their appropriate level. So petitions from the 'British merchants' required and received much more consideration than formerly. The Loyalists had not yet had time to start in business. All their energies were needed in hewing out their future homes. But two parts of the American Republic, Vermont and Kentucky, were very anxious to do business with the British at any reasonable price. Some of their citizens were even ready for a change of allegiance if the terms were only good enough. Vermont wanted a 'free trade' outlet to the St Lawrence by way of the Richelieu. The rapids between St Johns and Chambly lay in British territory. But Vermont was ready to join in building a canal and would even become British to make sure. The old Green Mountain Boys had changed their tune. Ethan Allen himself had buried the hatchet and, like his brother, become Carleton's friendly correspondent. He frankly explained that what Vermonters really wanted was 'property not liberty' and added that they would stand no coercion from the American government. About the same time Kentucky was bent on getting an equally 'free trade' outlet to the Gulf of Mexico by way of the Mississippi. The fact that France Spain, the British Empire, and the United States might all be involved in war over it did not trouble the conspirators in the least. The central authority of the new Republic was still weak. The individual states were still ready to fly asunder. Federal taxation was greatly feared. Anything that savoured of federal interference with state rights was passionately resented. The general spirit of the westerners was that of the exploiting pioneer in a virgin wilderness—a law unto itself alone. There were various plans for opening the coveted Mississippi. One was to join Spain. Another was to seize New Orleans, turn out the French, and bring in the British. Then, to make the plot complete, the French minister to the United States was asking permission to make a tour through Canada at the very time when Carleton was sending home reams of documents bearing on the impending troubles. The letters exchanged on this subject are perfect models of politeness. But Carleton's answer was an emphatic No.

Foreign complications were thickening fast. The French Revolution had already begun, though its effect was not yet felt in Canada. The American government was anxiously watching its refractory states, while an anti-British political party was making headway in the South. As if this was not enough to engage whatever attention Carleton had to spare from the internal affairs of Canada, he suddenly heard that the Spaniards had been seizing British vessels trading to a British post on Vancouver Island. [Footnote: *See Pioneers of the Pacific Coast* in this Series.] This Nootka Affair, which nearly brought on a war with Spain in 1790, was settled in London and Madrid. But the threat of war added to Carleton's anxieties.

Meanwhile the governor was busily employed with an immigration problem. It was desirable that the English-speaking immigrants should settle on the land with the least possible friction between them and the French Canadians. The French Canadians differed among themselves. But no such differences brought them any closer to their new neighbours on questions of land settlement. The French had granted lands in seigneuries. The British would hear of nothing but free and common socage. French farms were measured by the arpent and were staked out in long and narrow oblongs. British farms were measured by the acre and staked out 'on the square. ' Language, laws, religion, manners and customs, ways of life, were also different. So there was hardly any intermixture of settlements. The French Canadians remained where they were. Most of the new Anglo-Canadians settled in the Maritime Provinces or moved west into what is now Ontario. A few settled in rural Quebec on lands outside the line of seigneuries. The Eastern Townships, that part of the province lying east of the Richelieu and nearest the American frontier, absorbed many English, Irish, and Scots, as well as a good many Americans who were attracted by cheap land. Ontario, or Upper Canada, received still more Americans, who were to be a thorn in the side of the British during the War of 1812.

But Carleton's work comprised much more than this. There were the Church of England, the Post Office, a refractory lieutenant-governor down in Prince Edward Island, two royal visitors, and many other distracting matters. The only Anglican see thus far established was at Halifax; but the bishop there had authority over the whole country and the government intended to establish the Church of England in Canada and endow it. The Presbyterians also petitioned for the establishment of the Scottish Church. The fortunes or misfortunes of the Clergy Reserves belong to another chapter of Canadian history. But the root of their good or evil was planted in the time of Carleton. The postal service was surrounded by enormous difficulties—the vast extent of wild country, the few towns, the long winters, the poverty of the people. The question of the winter port was even then a live one between St John and Halifax. Each of these towns asserted its advantages and promised twelve trips a year and connection with Quebec overland by means of walking postmen till a bush road should be cut from Quebec to the sea. In Prince Edward Island the old lieutenant-governor, Walter Patterson, declined to make way for the new one, Edmund Fanning. In the end Patterson gave up the contest. But the incident, trivial as it now appears, shows what a governor-general had to face in the early days when each province had queer little ways of its own. Patterson had no precise official reason. But he said he could not go home to answer charges he did not understand and leave an island which had been his very successful hobby for so many years! The people sided with him so vigorously that time had to be given them to cool down before the transfer could be peaceably effected.

A judge whose court is in perpetual session or a commander whose inadequate forces are continually surrounded by prospective enemies has little time for the amenities of purely social life. So Carleton generally left his young consort to rule the viceregal court at the Chateau St Louis with a perfect blend of London and Versailles. Two Princes of the Blood, however, demanded more than the usual attention from the governor. Prince William Henry, afterwards King William IV, was the first member of the Royal Family to set foot in the New World when he arrived in H. M.S. *Pegasus* in 1787. He was the proverbial jolly Jack Tar, extremely affable to everybody; and he quickly won golden opinions from all who met him, except perhaps from Lady Dorchester and sundry would-be partners for his duty dances. Philippe Aubert de Gaspe and other privileged chroniclers record with slightly shocked delight how often he would break loose from Lady Dorchester's designing care, long before she thought it right for him to do so, and 'command' his partners for their pretty faces instead of by precedence. At Sorel the people were so carried away by their enthusiasm that they insisted on changing the name of their little town to William Henry. Happily this name never took root in public sentiment and the old one soon came back to stay.

The second member of the Royal Family to come to Canada was Prince Edward, Duke of Kent, fourth son of George III, father of Queen Victoria and grandfather of Prince Arthur, Duke of Connaught, who became the first royal governor-general in 1911, exactly a hundred and twenty years later. The Duke of Kent would have gladly returned to Quebec as governor-general, and the people would have gladly welcomed him. But he was not a favourite with the government at home, and so he never came. There was no doubt about his being a popular favourite in Quebec during the three years he spent there as colonel of the 7th Fusiliers. Nor has he been forgotten to the present day. Kent House is still the name of his quarters in the town as well as of his country residence at Montmorency Falls seven miles away, while the only new opening ever made in the walls is called Kent Gate.

The duke made fast friends with several of the seigneurial families, more especially with the de Salaberrys, whose manor-house at Beauport stood half-way between Montmorency and Quebec and not far from Montcalm's headquarters in 1759. The de Salaberrys were a military family. All the sons went into the Army and one became the hero of Chateauguay in the War of 1812. But the duke mixed freely with many other people than the local aristocracy. He was young, high-spirited, and loved adventure, as was proved by his subsequent gallantry at Martinique. He was also fond of driving round incognito, a habit which on at least one occasion obliged him to put his skill at boxing to good use. This was at Charlesbourg, a village near Quebec, where he was watching the fun at the first election ever held. Perhaps, from a meticulously constitutional point of view, the scene of a hotly contested election was not quite the place for Princes of the Blood. But, however that might be, when the duke saw two electors pommelling a third, who happened to be a friend of his, he dashed in to the rescue and floored both of them with a neatly planted right and left. One of these men, who lived to see King Edward VII arrive in 1860, as Prince of Wales, always took the greatest pride in telling successive generations of voters how Queen Victoria's father had knocked him down.

Like his brother before him the duke was very fond of dancing, and kept many a reluctant senior and many a tired-out chaperone up till all hours at the grand ball given in honour of his twenty-fourth birthday. Also like his brother he was inclined to reduce his duty dances to a minimum, much to Lady Dorchester's dismay. She had gone home with her husband for two years shortly after the duke's arrival. But she had seen enough of him, and was to see enough again on her return, to make her regret the good old times of more exacting ceremony. To her dying day, half a century later, she kept up a prodigious stateliness of manner. Before meals she expected the whole company to assemble and remain standing till she had made her royal progress through the room. She was a living anachronism for many years before her death, with her high-heeled, gold-buttoned, scarlet-coloured shoes, her Marie-Antoinette *coiffure* raised high above her head and interlaced with ribbons, her elaborately gorgeous dress, her intricate array of ornaments, and her long, jet-black, official-looking cane. But she was no anachronism to herself; for she still lived in the light of other days, in the fondly remembered times when, as the vice-reine of the Chateau St Louis, she helped her consort to settle nice points of etiquette and maintain a dignity befitting His Majesty's chosen representative. How did the seigneurs rank among themselves and with the leading English-speaking people? Who were to dance in the state minuet? Should dancing cease when the bishops came in, and for how long? Was that curtsy dropped quite low enough to her viceregal self, and did that *debutante* offer her blushing cheek in quite the proper way to Carleton when he graciously gave her the presentation kiss? How immeasurably far away it all seems now, that stately little court where the echoes of a dead Versailles lived on for seven years after the fall of the Bastille! And yet there is still one citizen o Quebec whose early partners were chaperoned by ladies who had danced the minuet with Lord and Lady Dorchester.

The two royal visits were not without their political significance — using the word political in its larger meaning. But the three years between them — that is, 1788-89-90 — formed the really pregnant time of constitutional development, when the Canada Act of 1791 was taking shape in the minds of its chief authors — Carleton and Smith in Canada, Grenville and Pitt in England. The Loyalists and the English-speaking merchants of Quebec and Montreal took good care to make themselves heard at every stage of the proceedings. Most French Canadians would have preferred to be left without the suspected blessings of a parliament. The clergy and seigneurs wished for a continuance of the Quebec Act, and the habitants wanted they knew not what, provided it would enable them to get more and give less. The English-speaking people, on the other hand, were all for a parliament. But they differed widely as to what kind of parliament would suit their purpose best. As a rule they acquiesced, with a more or less bad grace, in the necessity of admitting French Canadians on the same terms as themselves. If Canada, without the Maritime Provinces, should be taken as a whole then the French Canadians would only be in a moderate majority. If, however, two provinces, Upper Canada and Lower Canada, were to be erected, then the English-speaking minority in Lower Canada would be outvoted three or four to one.

There was a third alternative: no less than the establishment of a regular Dominion of British North America in 1790, a step which might have saved much trouble between that time and the Confederation of 1867. William Smith was its strongest advocate, Carleton its most cautious and judicious supporter. The chief justice was in favour of federating Upper and Lower Canada with the Maritime Provinces and Newfoundland into a single dominion. Each of the six provinces would have its own parliament under a lieutenant-governor, while there would also be a central parliament under a governor-general. Carleton forwarded the suggestion to the home government; but he nowhere committed himself to any very definite scheme. His own preference was for keeping the existing province of Quebec a little longer, then dividing it, and afterwards drawing in the other provinces. The chief justice preferred to make a constitution. The governor preferred to let it grow. The home government's preference could not be stated better than in Grenville's dispatch to Carleton of the 20th of October 1789: 'The general object is to assimilate the constitution to that of Great Britain as nearly as the difference arising from the manners of the People and from the present situation of the Province will admit.... Attention is due to the prejudices and habits of the French Inhabitants and every caution should be used to continue to them the enjoyment of those civil and religious Rights which were secured to them by the Capitulation or which have since been granted by the liberal and enlightened spirit of the British Government. ' Except for its rather too self-righteous conclusion this confidential announcement really is an admirable statement of the 'liberal and enlightened' views which prevailed at Westminster.

The bill, postponed in 1790, was introduced by Pitt himself in the House of Commons on the 7th of March 1791. Sixteen days later Adam Lymburner, a representative merchant of Quebec, whom Carleton described as 'a quiet, decent man, not unfriendly to the administration, ' pleaded for hours before the committee of the House of Commons against the division of the province. All the English-speaking minority in the prospective province of Lower Canada were afraid of being swamped by the French-Canadian vote, and so of being hampered in liberty and trade. The London merchants naturally backed Lymburner. Fox opposed the bill as not being liberal enough. Burke flared up into the speech which led to his final breach with Fox. Pitt, the pilot who was to weather far greater storms in the years to come, eventually got the bill through both Houses with substantial majorities. On the 14th of May it became law. Quebec and Ontario were parted for good, notwithstanding the legislative union of fifty years later.

The Canada Act, or, as it is better known, the Constitutional Act, cut off Upper Canada. Lower Canada was now the old Quebec reduced to its right size, endowed with clarified laws and a brand-new parliament, and made as acceptable as possible to the English-speaking minority without any injustice to the vastly greater French majority. Quebec, Three Rivers, Montreal, and Sorel got each two members in the new parliament, an allotment which ensured a certain representation of the 'British' merchants. The franchise was the same in both provinces: in the country parts a forty-shilling freehold or its equivalent, and in the towns either a five-pound annual ownership value or twice that for a tenant. The Crown gave up all taxation except commercial duties, which were to be applied solely for the benefit of the provinces. Lands outside the seigneuries were to be in free and common socage, while seigneurial tenure itself could be converted into freehold on petition. One-seventh of the Crown lands was reserved for the endowment of the Church of England. The Crown kept all rights of veto and appointment. The legislatures were small in membership. The Upper Houses could be made hereditary; though the actual tenure was never more than for life during good behaviour. Carleton favoured the hereditary principle whenever it could be applied with advantage. But he knew the ups and downs of colonial fortunes too well to believe that Canada was ready for any such experiment.

No one dreamt of having what is now known as responsible government, that is, an executive sitting in the legislature and responsible to the legislature for its acts. Nor was the greatest of all parliamentary powers—the power of the purse—given outright. This, however, was owing to simple force of circumstances and not to any desire of abridging the liberties of the people. The fact is that at this time eighty per cent of the total civil expenditure had to be paid by the home government. It is frequently ignored that the mother country paid most of Canada's bills till long after the War of 1812, that she paid nearly all the naval and military accounts for longer still, and that she has borne far more than her own share of the common defence down to the present day.

The new constitution came into force on the 26th of December 1791; and, for the first time, Upper and Lower Canada had the right to elect their own representatives. Assemblies, of course, were nothing new in British North America. Nova Scotia had an assembly in 1758, the year that Louisbourg was taken. Prince Edward Island had one in 1773, the year before the Quebec Act was passed. New Brunswick had one in 1786, the year Carleton began his second term. But assemblies still had all the charm of novelty in 'Canada proper. ' Perhaps it would be more appropriate to say that Upper Canada experienced more charm than novelty while Lower Canada experienced more novelty than charm. The Anglo-Canadians in all five provinces were used to parliaments in America. Their ancestors had been used to them for centuries in England. So the little parliament of Upper Canada at Newark passed as many bills in five weeks as that of Lower Canada passed in seven months. The fact that there were fifty members in the Assembly at Quebec, while there were only half as many in both chambers at Newark, doubtless had something to do with it. But the fact that the Quebec parliament was an innovation, while the one at Newark was a simple development, had very much more.

There is no need to follow the course of legislation in any of the five provinces. As most of the civil and practically all the naval and military expenditure had to be met by the Imperial Treasury, and as Canada was five parts and no whole from her own parliamentary point of view, the legislation required for a grand total of two hundred and fifty thousand people could not be of the national kind. But at Quebec the scene, the setting, and the unheard-of innovation itself all give a special interest to every detail of the opening ceremony on the 17th of December 1792.

Carleton was in England, so the Speech from the Throne was read by the lieutenant-governor, Major-General Sir Alured Clarke. Half of the Upper House and two-thirds of the Lower were French Canadians. A French-Canadian member was nominated for the speakership and elected unanimously. Both races were for the most part represented by members whose official title of 'Honourable Gentlemen' was not at all a misnomer. The French members of the Assembly were half distrustful both of it and of themselves. But they knew how to add grace and dignity to a very notable occasion. The old Bishop's Palace served as the Houses of Parliament and so continued for many years to come. It was a solid rather than a stately pile. But it stood on a commanding site at the head of Mountain Hill between the Grand Battery and the Chateau St Louis. Every one was in uniform or in what corresponded to court dress. Round the throne stood many officers in their red and gold, conspicuous among them the Duke of Kent. In front sat the Executive and Legislative Councillors, corresponding to the modern cabinet ministers and senators. Their roll, as well as the Assembly's, bore many names that recalled the glories of the old regime—St Ours, Longueuil, de Lanaudiere, Boucherville, de Salaberry, de Lotbiniere, and many more. The Council chamber was crowded in every part long before the governor arrived. 'The Ladies introduced into the House' were 'without Hat, Cloak, or Bonnet, ' the 'Doorkeeper of His Majesty's Council' having taken good care to see them 'leave the same in the Great Committee Room previous to their Introduction. ' 'The Ladies attached to His Excellency's Suite' were admitted 'within the railing or body of the House' and 'accommodated with the seats of the members as far as possible. ' Outwardly it was all very much the same in principle as the opening of any other British parliament—the escort, guard, and band, the royal salute, the brilliant staff, the scarlet cloth of state, the few and quiet members of the Upper House, the many of the Lower, jostling each other to get a good place near Mr Speaker at the bar, the radiant ladies, the crowded galleries corniced with inquiring faces and craned necks, the Gentlemen Ushers and their quaint bows, the Speech from the Throne and the occasional lifting of His Excellency's hat, the retiring in full state; and then the ebbing away of all the sightseers, their eddying currents of packed humanity in the halls and passages, the porch, the door, the emptying street. But inwardly what a world of difference! For here was the first British parliament in which legislators of foreign birth and blood and language were shaping British laws as British subjects.

In September 1793 Carleton returned from his two years' absence and was welcomed more warmly than ever. Quebec blazed with illuminations. The streets swarmed with eager crowds. The first session of the first parliament had been better than any one had dared to hope for. There was a general tendency to give the new constitution a fair trial; and all classes looked to Carleton to make the harmony that had been attained both permanent and universal. Dr Jacob Mountain, first Anglican bishop of Quebec, also arrived shortly afterwards and was warmly greeted by the Roman Catholic prelate, who embraced him, saying, 'It's time you came to shepherd your own flock. ' Mountain was statesman and churchman in one. He had been chosen by the elder Pitt to be the younger's tutor and then chosen by the younger to be his private secretary. The fact that the Anglican bishop of Quebec was then and for many years afterwards a sort of Canadian chaplain-general to the Imperial troops and that most of the leading officials and leading Loyalists belonged to the Church of England made him a personage of great importance. It was fortunate that, as in the case of Inglis down in Halifax, the choice could not have fallen on a better man or on one who knew better how to win the esteem of communions other than his own. This same year (1793) died William Smith, full of honours. But the next year his excellent successor arrived in the person of William Osgoode, the new chief justice, an eminent English lawyer who had served for two years as chief justice of Upper Canada and whose name is commemorated in Osgoode Hall, Toronto. He had come out on the distinct understanding that no fees were to be attached to his office, only a definite salary. This was a great triumph for Carleton, who certainly practised what he preached.

So far, so good. But the third conspicuous new arrival, John Graves Simcoe, lieutenant-governor of Upper Canada, who had come out the year before, was a great deal less to Carleton's liking. Simcoe was a good officer who threw himself heart and soul into the work of settling the new province. He won the affectionate regard of his people and is gratefully remembered by their posterity. But he was too exclusively of his own province in his civil and military outlook and was disposed to ignore Carleton as his official chief. Moreover, he was appointed in spite of Carleton's strongly expressed preference for Sir John Johnson, who, to all appearances, was the very man for the post. Sir William Johnson, the first baronet, had been the great British leader of the Indians and a person of much consequence throughout America. His son John inherited many of his good qualities, thoroughly understood the West and its problems, was a devoted Loyalist all through the Revolution, when he raised the King's Royal Regiment of New York, and would have been second only to Carleton himself in the eyes of all Canadians, old and new. But the government thought his private interests too great for his public duty—an excellent general principle, though misapplied in this particular case. At any rate, Simcoe came instead, and the friction began at once. Simcoe's commission clearly made him subordinate to Carleton. Yet Simcoe made appointments without consulting his superior and argued the point after he had been brought to book. He communicated directly with the home government over his superior's head and was not rebuked by the minister to whom he wrote—Henry Dundas, afterwards first Viscount Melville. Dundas, indeed, was half inclined to snub Carleton. Simcoe desired to establish military posts wherever he thought they would best promote immediate settlement, a policy which would tend to sap both the government's resources and the self-reliance of the settlers. He also wished to fix the capital at London instead of York, now Toronto, and to make York instead of Kingston the naval base for Lake Ontario. Thus the friction continued. At length Carleton wrote to the Duke of Portland, Pitt's home secretary, saying: 'All command, civil and military, being thus disorganized and without remedy, your Grace will, I hope, excuse my anxiety for the arrival of any successor, who may have authority sufficient to restore order, lest these insubordinations should extend to mutiny among the troops and sedition among the people. ' That was in November 1795. The government, however, took no decisive action, and next year both Carleton and Simcoe left Canada for ever.

When this unfortunate quarrel began (1793) Canada was in grave danger of being attacked by both the French and the American republics. The danger, however, had been greatly lessened by Jay's Treaty of 1794 and was to be still further lessened (1796) by the transfer of the Western Posts to the United States and by the presidential election which gave the Federal party a new lease of power, though no longer under Washington. Had Carleton remained in Canada these felicitous events would have offered him a unique opportunity of strengthening the friendly ties between the British and the Americans in a way which might have saved some trouble later on. But that was not to be.

To understand the dangers which threatened Canada during the last three years of Carleton's rule we must go back to February 1793, when revolutionary France declared war on England and there then began that titanic struggle which only ended twenty-two years later on the field of Waterloo. The Americans were divided into two parties, one disposed to be friendly towards Great Britain, the other unfriendly. The names these parties then bore must not be confused with those borne by their political offspring at the present day. The Federals, progenitors of the present Republicans, formed the friendly party under Washington, Hamilton, and Jay. The Republicans, progenitors of the present Democrats, formed the unfriendly party under Jefferson, Madison, and Randolph. The Federals were in power, the Republicans in opposition. When the Republicans got into power in 1801 under Jefferson they pursued their anti-British policy till they finally brought on the War of 1812 under the presidency of Madison. The strength of the peace party lay in the North; that of the war party lay in the South. The peaceful Federals, now that Independence had been gained, were in favour of meeting the amicable British government half-way. When Pitt came into power in 1783 he at once held out the olive branch. Now, ten years later, the more far-seeing statesmen on both sides were preparing to confirm the new friendship in the practical form of Jay's Treaty, which put the United States into what is at present known as a most-favoured-nation position with regard to British trade and commerce. Moreover, Washington and his Northern Federals much preferred a British Canada to a French one, while Jefferson and the Southern Republicans thought any stick was good enough to beat the British dog with.

The Jeffersonians eagerly seized on the reports of a speech which Carleton made to the Miamis, who lived just south of Detroit, and used it to the utmost as a means of stirring up anti-British feeling. Carleton had said: 'You are witnesses that we have acted in the most peaceable manner and borne the language and conduct of the United States with patience. But I believe our patience is almost exhausted. ' Applied to the vexed questions of the Western Posts, of the lawless ways of the exterminating American pioneers, and of the infinitely worse jobbing politicians behind them, this language was mildness itself. But in view of the high statesmanship of Washington and his government it was injudicious. All the same, Dundas, more especially because he was a cabinet minister, was even more injudicious when he adopted a tone of reproof towards Carleton, whose great services, past and present, entitled him to unusual respect and confidence. The negotiations for Jay's Treaty were then in progress in London, and Jefferson saw his chance of injuring both the American and British governments by magnifying Carleton's speech into an 'unwarrantable outrage. ' He also hoped that an Indian war would upset the treaty and bring on a British war as well. And the prospect did look encouragingly black in the West, where the American general Wayne was ready waiting south of Lake Erie, while the trade in scalps was unusually brisk. Forty dollars was the regular market price for an ordinary Indian's scalp. But as much as a thousand was offered for Simon Girty's in the hope of getting that inconvenient British scout put quickly out of the way. Nearer home Jefferson and his band of demagogues had other arguments as well. The Federal North would suffer most by war, while the Republican South might use war as a means of repudiating all the debts she owed to Englishmen. This would have been a very different thing from the insolvency of the Continental Congress during the Revolution. It was dire want, not financial infamy, that made the Revolutionary paper money 'not worth a Continental. ' But it would have been sheer theft for the Jeffersonian South to have made its honest obligations 'rotten as a Pennsylvanian bond. '

The wild French-Revolutionary rage that swept through the South now fanned the flame and made the sparks fly over into Canada. In April 1793 a fiery Red Republican, named Genet, landed at Charleston as French minister to the United States and made a triumphal progress to Philadelphia. Nobody bothered about the fundamental differences between the French and American revolutions. France and England were going to war and that was enough. Genet was one of those 'impossibles' whom revolutions throw into ridiculous power. When he began his campaign the Republican South was at his feet. Planters and legislators donned caps of liberty and danced themselves so crazy over the rights of abstract man that they had no enthusiasm left for such concrete instances as Loyalists, Englishmen, and their own plantation slaves. Then Genet made his next step in the new diplomacy by fitting out French privateers in American harbours and seizing British vessels in American waters. This brought Washington down on him at once. Then he lost his head completely, abused everybody, including Jefferson, and retired from public life as an American citizen, being afraid to go home.

Genet's absurd career was short, but very meteoric while it lasted, and full of anti-British mischief-making. His agents were everywhere; and his successor, Adet, carried on the underground agitation with equal zeal and more astuteness. Vermont offered an excellent base of operations. Finding that its British proclivities had not produced the Chambly canal for its trade with the St Lawrence, it had become more violently anti-British than ever before and even proposed taking Canada single-handed. This time its new policy remained at fever heat for over three years and only cooled down when a British man-of-war captured the incongruously named *Olive Branch*, in which Ira Allen was trying to run the blockade from Ostend with twenty thousand muskets and other arms which he represented as being solely for the annual drill of the Vermont militia. Thus Carleton had to watch the raging South, the dangerous West, and bellicose Vermont, all together, besides taking whatever measures he could against the swarms of secret enemies within the gates. The American immigrants who wanted 'property not liberty' were ready enough for a change of flag whenever it suited them. But they were few compared with the mass of French Canadians who were being stirred into disaffection. The seigneurs, the clergy, and the very few enlightened people of other classes had no desire for being conquered by a regicide France or an obliterating American Republic. But many of the habitants and of the uneducated in the towns lent a willing ear to those who promised them all kinds of liberty and property put together.

The danger was all the greater because it was no longer one foreigner intriguing against another, as in 1775, but French against British and class against class. Some of the appeals were still ridiculous. The habitants found themselves credited with an unslakable thirst for higher education. They were promised 'free' maritime intercommunication between the Old World and the New, a wonderful extension of representative institutions, and much more to the same effect, universal revolutionary brotherhood included. But when Frenchmen came promising fleets and armies, when these emissaries were backed by French Canadians who had left home for good reasons after the troubles of 1775, and when the habitants were positively assured by all these credible witnesses that France and the United States were going to drive the British out of Canada and make a heaven on earth for all who would turn against Carleton, then there really was something that sensible men could believe. Everything for nothing—or next to nothing. Only turn against the British and the rest would be easy. No more tithes to the cures, no more seigneurial dues, no more taxes to a government which put half the money in its own pocket and sent the other half to the king, who spent it buying palaces and crowns.

'Nothing is too absurd for them to believe, wrote Carleton, who felt all the old troubles of 1775 coming back in a greatly aggravated form. He lost no time in vain regrets, however, but got a militia bill through parliament, improved the defences of Quebec, and issued a proclamation enjoining all good subjects to find out, report, and seize every sedition-monger they could lay their hands on. An attempt to embody two thousand militiamen by ballot was a dead failure. The few English-speaking militiamen required came forward 'with alacrity. ' The habitants hung back or broke into riotous mobs. The ordinary habitant could hardly be blamed. He saw little difference between one kind of English-speaking people and another. So he naturally thought it best to be on the side of the prospective winners, especially when they persuaded him that he would get back everything taken from him by 'the infamous Quebec Act. ' There really was no way whatever of getting him to see the truth under these circumstances. The mere fact that his condition had improved so much under British rule made him all the readier to cry for the Franco-American moon. Things presently went from bad to worse. A glowing, bombastic address from 'The Free French to their Canadian Brothers' (who of course were 'slaves') was even read out at more than one church door. Then the Quebec Assembly unanimously passed an Alien Act in May 1794, and suspected characters began to find that two could play at the game. This stringent act was not passed a day too soon. By its provisions the Habeas Corpus Act could be suspended or suppressed and the strongest measures taken against sedition in every form. Monk, the attorney-general, reported that 'It is astonishing to find the same savagery exhibited here as in France. ' The habitants and lower class of townsfolk had beers well worked up 'to follow France and the United States by destroying a throne which was the seat of hypocrisy, imposture, despotism, greed, cruelty' and all the other deadly sins. The first step was to be the assassination of all obnoxious officials and leading British patriots the minute the promised invasion began to prove successful.

No war came. And, as we have seen already, Carleton's last year, 1796, was more peaceful than his first. But even then the external dangers made the governor-general's post a very trying one, especially when internal troubles were equally rife. Thus Carleton never enjoyed a single day without its anxious moments till, old and growing weary, though devoted as ever, he finally left Quebec on the 9th of July. This was the second occasion on which he had been forced to resign by unfair treatment at the hands of those who should have been his best support. It was infinitely worse the first time, when he was stabbed in the back by that shameless political assassin, Lord George Germain. But the second was also inexcusable because there could be no doubt whatever as to which of the incompatibles should have left his post—the replaceable Simcoe or the irreplaceable Carleton. Yet as H. M.S. *Active* rounded Point Levy, and the great stronghold of Quebec faded from his view, Carleton had at least the satisfaction of knowing that he had been the principal saviour of one British Canada and the principal founder of another.

CHAPTER X

'NUNC DIMITTIS' 1796-1808

Our tale is told.

The *Active* was wrecked on the island of Anticosti, where the estuary of the St Lawrence joins the Gulf. No lives were lost, and the Carletons reached Perce in Gaspe quite safely in a little coasting vessel. Then a ship came round from Halifax and sailed the family over to England at the end of September, just thirty years after Carleton had come out to Canada to take up a burden of oversea governance such as no other viceroy, in any part of the world-encircling British Empire, has ever borne so long.

He lived to become a wonderful link with the past. When he died at home in England he was in the sixty-seventh year of his connection with the Army and in the eighty-fifth of his age. More than any other man of note he brought the days of Marlborough into touch with those of Wellington, though a century lay between. At the time he received his first commission most of the senior officers were old Marlburians. At the time of his death Nelson had already won Trafalgar, Napoleon had already been emperor of the French for nearly three years, and Wellington had already begun the great Peninsular campaigns. Carleton's own life thus constitutes a most remarkable link between two very different eras of Imperial history. But he and his wife together constitute a still more remarkable link between two eras of Canadian history which are still farther apart. At first sight it seems almost impossible that he, who was the trusted friend o Wolfe, and she, who learned deportment at Versailles in the reign of Louis Quinze, should together make up a living link between 1690, when Frontenac saved Quebec from the American Colonials under Phips, and 1867, when the new Dominion was proclaimed there. But it is true. Carleton, born in the first quarter of the eighteenth century, knew several old men who had served at the Battle of the Boyne, which was fought three months before Frontenac sent his defiance to Phips 'from the mouth of my cannon. ' Carleton's wife, living far on into the second quarter of the nineteenth century, knew several rising young men who saw the Dominion of Canada well started on its great career.

All Carleton's sons went into the Army and all died on active service. The fourth was killed in 1814 at Bergen-op-Zoom carrying the same sword that Carleton himself had used there sixty-seven years before. A picture of the first siege of Bergen-op-Zoom hangs in the dining-room of the family seat at Greywell Hill to remind successive generations of their martial ancestors. But no Carleton needs to be reminded of a man's first duty at the call to arms. The present holder of the Dorchester estates and title is a woman. But her son and heir went straight to the front with the cavalry of the first British army corps to take the field in Belgium during the Great World War of 1914.

Carleton spent most of his last twelve years at Kempshot near Basingstoke because he kept his stud there and horses were his chief delight. But he died at Stubbings, his place near Maidenhead beside the silver Thames, on the 10th of November 1808.

Thus, after an unadventurous youth and early manhood, he spent his long maturity steering the ship of state through troublous seas abroad; then passed life's evening in the quiet haven of his home.

BIBLIOGRAPHICAL NOTE

The Seigneurs and the Loyalists, both closely associated with Carleton's Canadian career, are treated in two volumes of the present Series: *The Seigneurs of Old Canada* and *The United Empire Loyalists*. Two other volumes also provide profitable reading: *The War Chief of the Six Nations: A Chronicle of Brant*, the Indian leader who was to Carleton's day what Tecumseh was to Brock's, and *The War Chief of the Ottawas: A Chronicle of the Pontiac War*.

Only one life of Carleton has been written, *Lord Dorchester*, by A. G. Bradley (1907). The student should also consult *John Graves Simcoe*, by Duncan Campbell Scott (1905), *Sir Frederick Haldimand*, by Jean McIlwraith (1904), and *A History of Canada from 1763 to 1812* by Sir Charles Lucas. Carleton is the leading character in the first half of the third volume of *Canada and its Provinces*, which, being the work of different authors, throws light on his character from several different British points of view as well as from several different kinds of evidence. Kingsford's *History of Canada*, volumes iv to vii, treats the period in considerable detail. Justin Smith's two volumes, *Our Struggle for the Fourteenth Colony*, is the work of a most painstaking American scholar who had already produced an excellent account of *Arnold's March from Cambridge to Quebec*, in which, for the first time, *Arnold's Journal* was printed word for word. *Arnold's Expedition to Quebec*, by J. Codman, is another careful work. These are the complements of the British books mentioned above, as they emphasize the American point of view and draw more from American than from British sources of original information. The unfortunate defect of *Our Struggle for the Fourteenth Colony* is that the author's efforts to be sprightly at all costs tend to repel the serious student, while his very thoroughness itself repels the merely casual reader.

So many absurd or perverting mistakes are still made about the life and times of Carleton, and a full understanding of his career is of such vital importance to Canadian history, that no accounts given in the general run of books—including many so-called 'standard works'—should be accepted without reference to the original authorities. Justin Smith's books, cited above, have useful lists of authorities; though there is no discrimination between documents of very different value. The original British diaries kept during Montgomery and Arnold's beleaguerment have been published by the Literary and Historical Society of Quebec in two volumes, at the end of which there is a very useful bibliography showing the whereabouts of the actual manuscripts of these and many other documents in English, French, and German. In addition to the American and British diarists who wrote in English there were several prominent French Canadians and German officers who kept most interesting journals which are still extant. The Dominion Archives at Ottawa possess an immense mass of originals, facsimiles, and verbatim copies of every kind, including maps and illustrations. The Dominion Archivist, Dr Doughty, has himself edited, in collaboration with Professor Shortt, all the *Documents relating to the Constitutional History of Canada from 1759 to 1791.*

The present Chronicle is based on the original evidence of both sides.

END

LaVergne, TN USA
19 November 2009
164674LV00003B/243/P